PAUSED

PAUSED

by

Stephanie Ellis

BRIGIDS GATE PRESS
Bucyrus, Kansas
www.brigidsgatepress.com

Printed in the United States of America

As always—to my husband Geraint and our children: Bethan, Dylan and
Rhonwen.

Content warnings are provided at the end of this book.

CHAPTER ONE

The day had been busy, his lab at the university hospital, a hive of activity filled with both standard testing and cutting-edge research. Alex allowed himself to sing along to the radio. What was that last one? 'Things can only get better'? He didn't even let the slowing of the traffic annoy him. When the cars finally came to a halt, he continued to hum. He turned his face to the warmth of the late afternoon sun shining in through his window.

The traffic had stopped alongside the park which formed part of the route for his early morning run. He was nearly home. The new mobile cell tower had become a landmark of his journey.

His thoughts turned back to Mathilde's funding request. Would that go through? She had a theory concerning the possible existence of a dormant primeval gene which could trigger hibernation in humans. An interesting concept. If such a thing were possible, wouldn't that be good for the planet and ease demand on resources? Not to mention give people the rest they so sorely needed! Might even save a few marriages!

Alex's gaze drifted from the tower and lazily took in his surroundings.

Then he noticed Sam Hayling, sitting on the bench, which was not unusual. That he was in the exact same position as earlier—when Alex had jogged past him—was odd. Ignoring the disapproving looks from his fellow drivers, Alex eased his car out of the stationary flow and parked half on the pavement.

"Sam?"

There was no response to his greeting. Just like this morning, though Alex had dismissed that as his simply not having heard him, his mind elsewhere.

"Sam?"

He was standing over him and still the man failed to react.

Alex crouched down to study him further. The man's pulse was steady, his skin tone normal. There was nothing out of the ordinary about him— apart from his complete lack of response…and that smell. The man had pissed himself, maybe more, from what he could detect. His body odour indicated he had been sweating heavily, and it had been a hot day, yet Sam still wore the same sweater and coat he had donned for his early morning walk. Or had it been from the previous evening?

Guilt crawled over Alex as he realised he had passed Sam on the bench—in exactly the same position the night before—when he'd had to nip out to the shop to get more milk. He'd thrown out a greeting then, too, but had not waited for any acknowledgement. The man couldn't have sat there all night, could he? An even closer inspection revealed a splatter of bird droppings running down the back of Sam's coat.

Alex pulled out his phone and dialled 999, sticking around until the ambulance came and Sam was safely en route to the hospital. As Alex made his way home, all of his good feelings vanished.

"Don't blame yourself," said Anwen, after he'd told her about their neighbour. "You're not the only one who walked past him."

"I know," said Alex. "But doesn't that say something about us, as people? That we are all so wrapped up in ourselves we don't see what's right in front of us? Come on, I told the ambulance crew we'd go and break the news to his wife, bring her to the hospital." It was his way of saying sorry to Sam.

"I'm surprised Beryl hadn't been hunting him down when he didn't return home," said Anwen, pulling on a light jacket against the chill beginning to roll in as the sun dropped in the sky.

"Probably had a row," said Alex, closing the door behind them.

"We'd have heard though, wouldn't we?"

She was right. Beryl and Sam's arguments were famous in the neighbourhood, their volume carrying several houses over.

Sam lived only two doors away on the opposite side of their leafy avenue. With some misgiving, Alex knocked at the door. The house remained silent. He tried again, more forceful this time. No answer.

Anwen moved around him and peered in through a gap between the curtains that covered the front window. "I can see someone in there. Come on…Sam gave you a key for emergencies; use it."

Alex was already fiddling with his keys, trying to find the right one. "I've got a really bad feeling about this."

Anwen nodded.

"Beryl!" Anwen's voice echoed along the hallway. "It's only us."

There was no answer.

Alex opened the door to the front room. One look at Beryl's unmoving position, her lack of awareness to anything and that same stink as Sam, and his stomach sank further. Anwen was already at her side, feeling her pulse, repeating her name. Alex called 999 for the second time that day.

Ten minutes later, flashing blue lights appeared outside the house. Alex let them in, quickly explaining Beryl's condition and its similarity to that of her husband who'd also been admitted to hospital.

"What could it be?" asked Anwen, as they locked up the house once the ambulance had left.

"I haven't the faintest," said Alex, genuinely perplexed. "They seem absolutely catatonic."

"Well, she'll be in the hospital in a bit and Sam is already there," said Anwen. "They're in good hands. They'll be sorted soon."

"Hope so," said Alex. "I'll check in with the doctors tomorrow. I dare say my lab will be involved with their testing." Whilst he was worried about his neighbours, he was also genuinely curious as to what could cause a human's body to shut off its reflex and response systems so completely.

He spent the rest of the evening idly watching television and trying to forget the couple for a little while. News about the rising share price for Hum Protocol PLC gave him a brief moment of relief. He'd bought in on the comms company a couple of years back when it was just starting up, on Sam's advice. Now, it was everywhere. Worldwide. *You'll make a killing,* Sam had said.

The vacant look in his neighbour's eyes kept returning to him. Alex had to admit, he was worried. His dreams about cashing in and retiring to some sun-drenched island vanished in an instant.

CHAPTER TWO

Alex skipped his morning jog, unable to take his mind off Sam and Beryl ever since they were admitted to hospital. Three weeks had passed and no one was any the wiser. It was getting harder and harder to summon up the energy, his sleep disturbed by visions of himself sitting there, unable to move, whilst crowds passed him by, his silent pleas for help unheard. Instead, he had a quick breakfast and was at his desk before his team arrived, scanning the day's testing schedule on his computer. Sam and Beryl's names appeared on the list, tagged with the name of their consulting doctor. An alert had also been attached, indicating the interest of the hospital's research director, Georgina Holland, in the case. He added his own name to the alert.

Continuing to fret, he picked up his tablet and made his way to the ward where the couple were being treated. It was a small bay with only two beds. The nurses were used to his daily visits to check on their mysterious case.

"Strange, isn't it, Dr. Griffiths?" A nurse had appeared behind him, moving around to start taking readings, adjust IVs, make sure the patients were comfortable. "Come up with anything in the lab yet?"

He shook his head. "We've done the standard tests. All have come back clear."

"Must've felt strange, seeing them like that. Human statues. Reminds me of those you see in the city centres, the ones who stand absolutely motionless for ages and then suddenly move. Frighten the life out of me, those do."

Alex had seen one like that recently in town, a silver painted astronaut. It was so still, so silent, until its head turned towards you. The effect was unnerving, and more than one child had been reduced to tears whilst older folk laughed at the foolishness of their reactions.

She replaced the clipboard and headed towards the door, pausing at his side. "Do they hear us? Are they aware of their surroundings?"

"Tests are indicating this is highly probable," he replied. "So—"

"So mind what we say and talk to them. Usual procedure?"

"Yes," he said. "And you know these two are friends of mine? Let me know as soon as there's any change?"

"Of course, Doctor," she said, giving him a sympathetic smile and leaving him to contemplate his neighbours alone.

As he turned to make his way back to his lab, his boss, Georgina "Georgie" Holland, entered the bay.

"Alex," she said. "I hear you know these two?"

"Yeah, neighbours."

"Unusual case," she said, standing aside to let two orderlies enter the room. "How well do you know them?"

Alex thought, despite everything, including their geographical closeness, he probably didn't know them that well after all. Their talks had always been superficial, not giving away anything too personal. Unlike Anwen, who'd had more than one heart to heart with Beryl—a basic difference between male and female friendships.

"Not as well as my wife did," he replied. "We exchanged small talk, helped each other out on occasion, had a pint down at the pub…but personal stuff, that's down to the wives. I've already asked her if Beryl mentioned not feeling well, but there was nothing. Anwen bumped into her in the corner shop the day before I found Sam, said she seemed fine. Nothing different about her at all."

Georgie nodded.

"You're moving them?" he asked, as the orderlies started manoeuvring the beds and attached equipment.

"Putting them in isolation," said Georgie. "Seems a few more have turned up with similar symptoms, and people are talking. Some of the staff are getting a bit anxious. I don't for one minute believe it's anything to worry about but best to tuck them out of sight until we know a bit more."

"How many?"

"Three. Another couple. Live over towards Shirley. And a toddler. The latter is of some concern—I mean, they all are, naturally, but the parents are being quite…um…vocal. Demanding answers *now*. Well, you can't blame them. It's what we would all do."

"When did they come in?"

"Only an hour ago," she said. "We need to fast track any tests on this group. I've had admissions send you their background."

"I'll look in on them before I get back to the lab," he said. "See if they can give me a clue."

He left her watching over the removal of his neighbours from their room and made his way to the isolation ward.

Alex opened a file on his tablet. The information Georgie had mentioned was already there. He opened the document. The couple were elderly, discovered by a distraught daughter who'd gone around after receiving no reply to her morning phone call. She would normally ring at breakfast and visit in the afternoons. The carers had said they were perfectly fine when they'd left them at 9:00 a.m. A lie, it turned out, as their daughter had visited the previous afternoon and, when she discovered them, they were sat exactly as she had left them, their clothes unchanged, although now somewhat soiled. The carers had skipped both evening and morning visits. Mr. and Mrs. Pierce had been catatonic for at least eighteen hours, if not more.

The toddler, Jamie Phelps, was a different matter. He had been happily playing with his toys after breakfast and then just stopped. There was no cry, no whimper, nothing. His parents had driven immediately to hospital on the advice of the 999 call-handler. They were in a side room with the Pierce's daughter waiting for an explanation, something they could not give.

He left as the orderlies pushing Sam and Beryl arrived. Worryingly, there were two more gurneys behind them. He made his way quickly back to the lab.

*****

His team's schedule was full. They had performed not just the standard drug tests for everything from cannabis to heroin to spice to legal highs, every possibility, no matter how outlandish, was to be looked at on Georgie's orders. Pretty much every documented pathogen, both viral and bacterial, was also to be tested for. It sent a shiver down his spine. *Did she know something he didn't?*

There was something he wasn't being told and it would take an astonishing amount of overtime to meet demand. He was not sure even that would be enough. They had finite resources, after all. He tried calling but received no answer, her secretary proving equally evasive. With a sigh, he rose from his seat and set off once more around the labyrinth of hospital wards and research labs.

"What is it?" he demanded, when he finally cornered his boss by a vending machine. She normally wasn't this elusive.

Georgie Holland swirled her coffee cup, staring into its dregs before draining the remnants and meeting Alex's gaze.

"We've been asked to keep it quiet," she said. "There've been a handful of similar cases all around the country, and not just here, but in other countries too. The government thinks there's something coming but don't want to cause a panic, want to give us time to work on it. We've managed that to a certain extent, been able to pick up the victims discreetly. The numbers were quite low to allow this to go relatively unnoticed."

Her pager buzzed and she vanished, preventing him from asking anymore questions.

CHAPTER THREE

Nic and Sian sat two seats back from Rosie on the bus home from school. The sisters managed to avoid her during the day, but there would always come a point when she homed in on one or other of them. A missile waiting to explode in their faces, the fallout horrible and public. It was Friday, however, and a weekend of respite awaited them.

Yet it wasn't any comfort to Nic that they weren't the only ones targeted by the girl. She was an out-and-out bitch to all and sundry. At least Rosie was in her last year, like Nic, and they would be going their separate ways. If she'd been a year younger it would have left Sian to deal with Rosie on her own, and Nic's younger sister would have found that extremely difficult to handle.

"At least she's by herself for once," whispered Sian.

"Yeah." The absence of Rosie's usual gang of misery was a surprise. Nic sensed a chance. The desire to get even bubbled up, payback time.

"Look, there's two of us and one of her. Why don't we get off when she does, talk to her, try and get her to stop?"

Sian looked at Nic as if she was crazy. Perhaps she was, but even six months more of her incessant bullying was too much to countenance. Nic wanted it to stop and stop now.

"She gets off and takes the footpath over the rec," said Nic. "No one will see us."

"Very cloak and dagger," said Sian, still looking unconvinced.

"Well, if it all goes wrong, I don't really want anyone to see," said Nic.

"Or film," said Sian, with feeling.

Both had been subjected to unfortunate uploads to various platforms, public shaming they had not been able to confide to their parents. Nic watched Rosie press the button, ping the bell to stop the bus. She remained in her seat.

"Not going after her then?" asked Sian, relief flooding her face.

"Yes," said Nic, "but we get off at the next stop. We can loop around quite quickly and catch her up. Getting off at the same stop would be a bit too obvious."

Nobody paid them any attention as they got off. They were almost the last of the school crowd, another blessing. Nic could see Rosie disappearing over the crest of the common.

"Come on," she said, nudging her sister, and broke into a jog. She trusted to Rosie's dawdling gait that they would soon catch up. It was relatively easy going on this part of the rec, a wide-open space which normally featured teens hurtling around on illegal mini-bikes or generally being a nuisance. The corner Rosie was heading for was more of a wilderness, full of brambles and high hedgerows, a place for illicit drugs, boozing, and uncomfortable sex. Other secrets they hadn't shared with their parents.

The two sped up, Nic not wanting to let Rosie get beyond the hedges, Sian, not wanting to lose Nic.

The older sister hurtled around the corner and came to a sudden stop, her younger sibling cannoning hard into her. Rosie stood in the middle of the footpath, hands on hips, staring at them.

"Thought you could put one over on me?" She stepped closer to Nic.

Nic frowned, they hadn't let their voices carry. The grass had muffled their tread.

Rosie grinned. "I'd stopped to check the signal on my phone and saw you two get off the bus. Wondered why you did that. So here we are. What *are* we going to do about it?" She took another step forward.

Nic could smell the mint on Rosie's breath, teeth grinding at the gum in her smirking mouth, the mouth Nic wanted to smack. Her hands clenched at her sides, fists balled, ready to lash out. Then Nic felt Sian's hand on her arm, her sister tugging her back. She glanced at Sian, annoyed at the distraction, saw the fear in her sister's eyes, which suddenly widened at something behind Nic.

She whipped around but too late. Rosie had landed a heavy blow to the side of her head, sending her spinning to the ground.

"You should know by now, you never mess with me," said Rosie, looking down at her. The smile had gone and there was a cold, hard expression on her face. "Time you were taught a proper lesson—both of you."

Nic managed a quick look at Sian. She looked ready to run but hadn't done so yet. She pushed herself back up, waiting for another blow as she did so. It didn't matter that Rosie was stronger. Nic had had enough. Even if she came off worse, she had an overwhelming urge to hit back, to punch and kick the cow, *hurt* her. The blow didn't come. Rosie had started to swing her foot, ready to put the boot in—and then stopped.

Nic stared up at her foe in astonishment. All life seemed to have fled from the girl. Rosie's eyes were fixed on Nic, but they had gone blank. She appeared totally unaware of anything around her, including Nic lying at her feet.

"Nic? What happened?" Sian was staring at Rosie but hadn't got any closer.

Nic reached up and tapped Rosie's hand. No response. Standing up, she moved so she stood right in her face. The girl's mouth was open, mid-chew. A fly buzzed past and landed on Rosie's tongue. She made no response. Tentatively, Nic prodded hard. Still nothing. A vicious pinch to her cheek. Nothing.

She turned and smiled at Sian. "Looks like we can get a bit of payback after all."

"What's wrong with her?" asked Sian.

Nic shrugged. "Drugs? She's always had a stash of weed on her. Probably spice. The one we had that talk about the other day. Stops people from functioning." She walked around Rosie who seemed precariously balanced. "Shouldn't worry, she'll be back to her horrible normal self soon enough. In the meantime, let's enjoy the moment."

A small part of her tried to tell her Rosie needed help. Nic didn't want to listen. Years of being at the receiving end had brought her to this point. She would never get another chance.

Sian moved closer, reassured Rosie wouldn't suddenly lash out. She gave Rosie a hesitant push. The girl toppled to the ground and Sian jumped back in shock, ready to run away should Rosie come to life.

There was still no reaction.

"Lucky for her she had a soft landing," said Nic, eyeing the mass of ferns Rosie had fallen into. A memory came back, of changing room showers and taunts, those photographs. Even now they continued to resurface, shared by the boys at school as part of the general 'banter.' She smiled and knelt down beside Rosie, started to strip her.

"What are you doing?" asked Sian.

"Only what she did to me," said Nic. "Let's see how she likes it."

"Would you really do that to another girl after what you went through?"

"No," said Nic. "Just Rosie. Besides, there's more than just me. You know that. She's been taking photos and videos for years. Turned it into a bit of a money-spinner from what I can gather. She even operates on commission."

"Why didn't you tell the teachers, Mum and Dad?"

Nic eyed her sister. "Seriously? Look, you don't have to be part of this, but keep a watch for me, will you?"

She turned back to pulling Rosie's hoodie off, then the t-shirt, jeans down. Rosie's flesh spilled out left, right, and centre. Nic rose to her feet and took a few shots, crossed Rosie's arms on her chest so she looked dead. It still wasn't enough. Not for all the shame and humiliation she had endured. She ignored Sian's pleading look and unhooked Rosie's bra.

"Don't worry," said Nic. "She can keep her knickers on." This wasn't said out of any sense of decency, more because her underwear looked as though it hadn't been washed for a week and she didn't want to touch her any more than she already had. She took more snaps, draped her arms and legs at different angles, Rosie proved surprisingly malleable.

"Enough," said Nic. "I've got what I need." She turned away.

"We can't leave her like that," said Sian. "We can't do that—even to her!"

Nic considered her foe. Sian was right. "Come on, then. Help me dress her."

Between them, they got Rosie into her clothes and then dragged her over to the base of a nearby trunk.

"We're leaving her?" asked Sian, still incredulous at her sister's actions.

"Yes," said Nic. "For a couple of hours, anyway. Then I'll pretend to discover her later, call an ambulance."

"I still don't like it," said Sian.

"You don't have to. But I can tell you one thing; if the positions were reversed, she wouldn't think twice about doing worse to us."

It was true. There would have been no re-dressing, no putting her in a position of relative safety. Rosie would've probably charged a viewing fee, a price to touch, or more, like she did a year ago to Shelley McKenzie when her drink had been spiked.

"Let's get home," she said. "We need to work on Mum and Dad about that party. Dad's on a mega guilt trip about working the past couple of weekends trying to find out what's wrong with old Sam and Beryl. It's our trump card if we play it right."

Nic led the way, Sian struggling to keep up with her sister's pace, both relieved to be leaving Rosie behind.

"You promise you'll make that call, won't you?" said Sian, puffing away behind her, the anxiety evident in her voice.

Nic had no such qualms. Karma could be a bitch.

CHAPTER FOUR

"The numbers *were* quite low?" Alex continued the previous day's conversation. He was not going to let Georgie off the hook that easily. He'd checked the hospital's admission records and found only a couple more added to the isolation ward. His contacts at other hospitals had yet to get back to him.

She sighed. "More and more are presenting in the same manner. And it's all so bloody sudden. Our medical teams at the government level have been in constant communication. They're trying to manage this better than that covid fiasco. Lessons learned and all that."

"Were?" persisted Alex.

"Some of these unfortunates have been falling into this state in public places. People are filming them, uploading to social media. It's going viral in more ways than one. We're expecting the national news to pick up on it anytime now—if they haven't already."

"Why would people film these victims?" asked Alex, perplexed. "I mean, they're not actually doing anything, are they?"

Georgie gave him a pitying look. "You never were one for Facebook or whatever, were you? People are cruel."

It reminded Alex of a recent news story of youths setting fire to a tramp sleeping on a park bench in Eastleigh. The man had died. Yes, there were some monsters out there.

"I think it might be useful if you saw some of these videos," said Georgie. "I've compiled a file with some that I've highlighted as of particular interest as they show, purely by chance, the moment catatonia strikes."

Alex wasn't sure he wanted to view these clips, but for the sake of being fully informed, there was no way of avoiding it. By the time he went home, he felt sickened by the nature of some of his fellow humans.

*****

"Phones away at dinner."
Nobody paid any attention.

Alex sighed, dreading the battleground family mealtimes had become. He didn't need this on top of everything else going on at work. He looked to his wife for support, but her eyes were also glued to the screen.

"You should see this," she said, finally sliding her mobile across to him. Her expression was one of shock.

"What—"

"Just watch."

He looked down and tapped the video, Anwen and their daughters watching him, roles now reversed. He knew what was coming. It was another one.

This time a youth was bending over to light a batch of fireworks, the flame flickering in his hand, shouts from his mates to get on with it. The lad froze just as the flame caught. The cheers were replaced by screams to hurry up, stop messing about. He didn't move and within seconds, the barrage exploded and he became an inferno.

Alex pushed both phone and plate away, his appetite gone.

"You think it's that spice stuff?" asked Anwen.

His wife had been following news reports about the latest 'zombie' drug, worried for their children. Seventeen and eighteen, they were slowly being allowed their freedom, but whilst the girls were chafing at the bit, his wife spent her time worrying. As he did. As all parents did.

He shook his head. Some of his colleagues considered a rogue batch had hit the streets, but he thought it was something else. The physiological shutdown was too immediate. The evening's press however had homed in on a drug being responsible, regardless of whether it was feasible for an octogenarian or pre-school toddler to be users. In the U.S., one group had claimed responsibility, saying they had poisoned food products across the world—they had activists in every continent—and unless their demands were met, they would not reveal the cause or the cure. The government responded with its standard rebuttal of blackmail, and the supermarkets started testing their goods. For what though, they couldn't—or wouldn't— say.

In the meantime, the families of those affected were providing lists of everything they knew their loved ones had drunk or eaten—as far as they were able. The Environment Agency was also doing its bit, but Alex felt they would all draw a blank. The affected group was too diverse. Something else was at play.

"Dad, there's more," said Nic, sliding her phone over. There was a tremor in her voice.

It was a continuation of the first video. Two youths rushing over to their burning friend, voices calling for an ambulance, others continuing to film. What sort of sick mind could do that? What person would just watch?

The lads held out a blanket to smother the flames—and then they froze. Flames leapt onto the blanket, advanced towards the youths. Neither of them moved or spoke. There were more screams. The image became blurry. He could hear the crackle of flames as they drew closer. Screams stopped, the only movement fire. The video stopped.

"They shouldn't put those videos up," said Anwen, her face pale. "It's not right."

"No," said Alex, in full agreement with the sentiment, "but it does show us what's happening. Might even help us work out what it is." He sounded like Georgie, becoming cold and clinical in response to the tragedies playing out in front of him. It was a necessary self-defence mechanism for him to be able to continue his work.

"Do you still have no idea?" asked Anwen.

"I haven't a clue," he said, reluctant to admit his team's failure, "but we're continuing to carry out tests on Sam and Beryl and those others they managed to get into hospital safely before they came to harm." He didn't say they were running out of tests to perform, that this was something beyond their experience. His wife looked anxious, but the girls' interest appeared to have already moved on, their earlier distress already compartmentalised, having become just another one of those things. A desensitisation which worried Alex. He tried to reassure himself it was merely their own coping mechanism.

"Better get ready," said Nic, getting up.

"Ready?" He looked from Anwen to the girls.

"Yeah, party tonight. Jules' eighteenth. You said we could go. Come on, it'll do us good. Stop us from thinking about this stuff. And it's Saturday—

not a school night!"

Nic knew which buttons to press.

Anwen smiled. "Yes, you go on now. Both of you and have a good time." She looked at Alex as they left the room. "At least Jules is only down the road."

He didn't answer. Sam and Beryl had *only* been down the road. He thought about work. The pressure on his lab team was building. People were expecting answers and fast.

CHAPTER FIVE

Peter Griffiths stared at his phone. He hadn't been in touch with his brother for ages, not since he and Alex had fallen out over Peter's—now ex—wife. Alex had been right about the woman, but Peter hadn't listened. Instead, he'd allowed her to take everything he had, including their son. At least he still had his shares in Hum. A birthday gift from Alex *after* the divorce. She'd been spitting chips about that when she found out.

It's about time, he thought. Someone had to make the first move and he missed Alex.

He started to tap on the screen when a call came through. His boss was bringing the date forwards for the demolition of the Three Sisters, the remaining chimney stacks standing over at Selford. Thankfully, the equipment and machinery had already been delivered and positioned. All it needed was the team.

Pete steeled himself for the abuse he would receive at the short-notice, answering each with the overtime figure quoted by his boss. His brother would have to wait a bit longer. He was probably busy anyway, chasing the elusive cure to the world's ailments. Their parents had done nothing but praise Alex, forgetting Pete in the process. It had been different when he was serving abroad in the army, the hero son. That all changed when he returned to civvy street.

The drive to the power plant was uneventful, very little traffic out this Sunday morning. The gloomy sky keeping many at home. The plant itself would have the usual full complement of staff. There was no such thing as weekend working in this industry, much like his service experience. After showing his pass at the gate, he drove another two miles to reach the chimneys demanding their attention. They were old stacks not far from a decommissioned reactor. Why they hadn't been demolished when the reactor was first built was something he couldn't figure out. Their demolition needed careful handling. Pete and his team were amongst the best, despite that they were currently waiting for him, casting somewhat sour looks his way after he'd parked and made his way over to greet them.

"Could think of better ways to be passing a Sunday morning," growled Finn, handing him his hard hat and hi-vis jacket.

"But would they pay as well?" asked Pete, hoping the money might focus them again.

Finn shrugged. "Maybe not, but it's a miserable bugger of a day to be fixing this regardless."

"Hangover?" Saturday night was always a heavy night for Finn. For most of them in truth, as it was one of the few days they did not have to abstain from the drink.

"Isn't it always?" piped up Tony. "Can't hold his beer anymore, can you, granddad?"

Finn aimed a slap at the back of the younger man's head, but he ducked, Finn's hand hitting nothing but air.

"Gonna test us then?" Bob nodded at the breathalyser lying in the back of the open work van.

Pete shook his head. "The boss said it wasn't needed today. I reckon he thinks we'd all fail and he'd never get the job done."

"Hope you got permission in writing," said Finn. "Wouldn't put it past the old bugger to screw us over if something goes wrong. Deny all knowledge like."

"I've recorded his call," said Pete. "Had a feeling he might cut a few corners."

"He might," said Bob, "doesn't mean to say we have to."

Pete studied his younger colleague. The man had three kids and another on the way. Not even thirty yet! He needed the money. "I test you and you're positive, you won't be able to work. Want to risk losing the bonus?"

Bob visibly slumped. "Nah, you're okay. We could do this job in our sleep. It's straightforward, isn't it?"

Despite their worrying surroundings, the job had already been earmarked as one of minimum effort for maximum price. Reactors were amongst the safest places these days, what with all the health and safety checks both worksite and employees were subjected to. The old chimney stacks they had been asked to remove showed no areas of weakness, nothing that could cause any problem. The men manoeuvred the machinery onto the platform, fixed the harnesses and their own, and looked expectantly at him. He took the hint and made his way to the cab of the crane. Normally he would be with the crew, but Stan hadn't been able to make it that morning. Pete was still legal. Just. His license would expire in a couple more days.

He groaned as he clambered into the cab, the small enclosed space at the base of the giant arm.

"It's like riding a bike," said his boss. "Once you've done it, you remember forever. Muscle memory."

Settling himself in place, he pulled on his seatbelt—*God knows why this was needed*, thought Pete, *they weren't going anywhere*—and gazed miserably at the panel. He tapped his phone and found the layout scheme sent by Stan. A few basic controls, that was all that was needed. Pretend it's one of your lad's video games, he'd typed. He was having a laugh. Pete was rubbish at those games, always lost, blown up or decapitated. Not something that would happen here, at least. He cast a quick look at his colleagues waiting patiently on the platform and gave them the thumbs up before pressing the ignition and using the levers to lift and guide the platform over the top of the chimney stack. To his surprise, he found his boss was right, the controls were easy, responded to the lightest touch and the onboard computer helped guide the arm with unerring accuracy. Computers were bloody everywhere these days. Already his team had turned away from him, were busy chatting to each other as they became smaller and smaller—flying ants.

The platform was above the stack, ready to be lowered over it to allow them to work on the uppermost reaches. The platform was a ring structure, the padding around the hole in its middle allowing friction to hold it in place around the outside of the stack. A miracle achieved only by accurate measurement of the circumference of the chimney.

He locked the crane's arm in position, allowing his colleagues to get on with their part of the job. The radio was on and he could hear their banter as they set the hydraulic equipment going and the steel jaws got to work nibbling at the bricks. Satisfied all was well, though he had no doubt Finn would be moaning about his head, he turned his thoughts back to his brother. He should talk to Alex. It had been too long. Pete diverted his attention from his workmates and typed out a quick text. No more than a

"Hello, how's it going?" but enough to break the ice, get a response. As soon as he pressed send, his hand began to tingle, the rest of his body following suit almost immediately. It was the strangest feeling he had ever experienced and then, just as he began to worry about it, it stopped.

Pete stared at his hand, the tremors which had accompanied the tingling, the sight of veins twitching beneath his skin had vanished. The surface of his flesh looked as calm and steady as ever. Probably some sort of static charge? It didn't matter. The feeling had been brief—unnerving, yes, but was done. Something to be forgotten.

"Pete. Pete! Answer, you bloody idiot!"

It was Bob, telling him they'd finished the first few metres of removal and needed to be lowered, *when his highness had time.*

A couple more manoeuvrings and the platform was sat in its new position, everything safe and secure as it should be, the broken rubble dropped down the central flue so it could be removed from the bottom. This method of demolition had become one of the safest devised.

He glanced at his phone on the dashboard. Its screen stayed blank. Alex hadn't answered yet. Probably on his way back from one of those morning jogs he always took. The runs Pete had always promised to join him on but never did.

His eye caught sight of the bulge of his stomach. The physique honed by his army days had long since vanished. Yeah, time to start running. Thoughts of a newer, improved Peter Griffiths drifted through his mind as he kept his eye lazily focussed on those above him. There were no other distractions to be sought, their worksite taped off to prevent any plant employees from drifting into danger.

A sharp pain stabbed behind his right eye, then his left, across his brow. *Not a migraine, not now*, he pleaded. He thought he'd beaten them, hadn't suffered one for years. The pressure continued to build, like a hammer pounding on an anvil, with the whole of his brain the forge. The feeling was so intense, he could no longer hold his head up. Instead, he cradled his skull in his hands, whimpering slightly as he did so. Then, just like the strange tingling experience, it was gone.

A quick look at his control panel and he saw no more than thirty seconds had passed, even though it had seemed a lot longer. He felt slightly woozy and took a quick drink of water, returning his attention to the platform. They were still working away up there, hadn't noticed anything wrong, thank goodness. The check-up his parents had been nagging at him to do finally seemed like a good idea. He'd get Alex to arrange it. His brother would be able to get him looked at relatively sharpish.

"Time to shift, Pete." Bob's voice came over the radio loud and clear. He sounded quite cheerful now.

"Okey doke, Bob." Pete put his bottle down and lifted his hand to start guiding the controls. As he grasped the lever, his sleeve cuff caught on something, directing his hand in a different direction than intended. He felt a vibration run through him as the unwanted command jarred the crane and the platform against the stack.

"Christ, Pete. What you playing at down there? Trying to give us a heart attack?" Bob's previous cheerfulness had morphed into annoyance.

Pete tried to speak. His mouth refused to open. He tried to lift his arm, disentangle his sleeve. It refused to obey. Nor could he move his head, his eyes fixed on the platform above where he could see his friends gesticulating at him. All the commands he sent from his mind to different parts of his body went ignored.

The platform crunched again.

"Shit, Pete. Stop playing silly buggers and get this fucking platform straight now!"

The crane continued to drift, directed by the continued pressure of his snagged arm. A total paralysis of his body had engulfed him, alongside an overwhelming terror that he could do nothing.

The control panel needed only the lightest touch. If such an incident had happened years ago, the machine would've come to a halt. Now however, it continued to respond to his slight pressure. Was anyone watching? Could anyone see?

He felt a strong vibration run through him as the crane pulled at the platform, the friction of the platform refusing to loosen its grip on the chimney, a bizarre tug of war. Both crane and platform had been built to the highest specification so the struggle between them should, in theory, come to an impasse and the movement would stop but…

As he watched the stack, he saw cracks appearing in the cement beneath the platform. If that gave—no, it didn't bear thinking about. It wouldn't happen. Bob was calling someone on his phone, as were the others, still screaming at him between jolts. Their increasingly anxious voices travelled to him over the radio. Someone would come soon, break into his cab, free him—and them.

The thought allowed him some calm, a moment of respite from the panic. His phone flashed, the screen lit up. He couldn't turn his head to see properly. Was it Alex? His boss? Fuck, he could do nothing. The grinding of machinery grew louder. Somewhere in the distance he heard sirens. The scream of an alarm echoed around him. He couldn't see his rescuers. They had to be close.

Initially angry, their shouts turned into terrified screams, howling at him, horror transmitted without a break.

"Fuck's sake, Pete. This isn't funny!"

"Pete! Oh my God, Pete…"

"Tony. Get that fucking harness back on, now."

"I can't, it won't. Pete!"

Another jolt and the platform tilted suddenly as a crack fissured around the side of the stack. Bob was tipped off the platform, dangling in the air, held by his safety harness. Tony wasn't so lucky. Pete could see him scrabbling as the platform tipped more, the fissure widening. The young man plummeted over the edge. Bloody fool always disconnected his harness despite their instructions; complained it got in the way of operating the rig up there. Pete could only watch, listening to his screams over the radio before there was a blast of static—and then nothing. With the refusal of his eyes to shift their focus, Pete was spared having to see the final landing. Nor did he hear any sound beyond what had been transmitted over the radio. The cab was fully soundproofed to protect the hearing of the driver.

Shadows flickered against the glass, reflections of emergency vehicles beginning to approach.

Then he felt the ground rumble, a vibration shearing up through his cab, as the impasse between the crane and the work platform came to an end. The stack beneath had weakened at the constant pressure and now tumbled beneath the platform which—finding itself suddenly free of its anchor—swung wildly, pounding against the reactor side, sending cracks along the structure. It swung another way and Pete briefly caught sight of his remaining three colleagues clinging precariously to the platform. Unable to turn his eyes from them, he followed the trajectory which was sending the crane and its burden towards a low building.

There were no screams, no words from his team.

He sent up every prayer he could that the unit contained nothing dangerous. The platform dropped, shearing away from the crane's cables. It crashed onto the structure, sending up a pile of dust and rubble as it split apart. There was a pause where for one merciful moment he felt a flicker of hope, and then came the flames. Explosions as something ignited amongst the destroyed mass. An inferno forced its way out of the unit, triggering other explosions. Fire danced its way towards him.

Other voices were shouting at him over the radio. His boss was there, begging, pleading with him to move, to get out. An emergency operator had also been patched in, was trying to get him to respond.

Didn't they realise it was useless? There was nothing anyone could do. Another explosion had caught the crane, was roaring up the side of his cab. He could feel the heat, its smothering presence invading his cab through the vents, followed by the fire itself. His phone's screen flashed again. Alex. The mobile's surface cracked and splintered. The dashboard began to melt and distort. Fire was claiming him from below. Up from under his seat, licking at his clothes, eating them quickly before starting to gorge themselves on his flesh. The pain was unbearable. He couldn't scream. Couldn't move. Couldn't escape. He could only watch as the world around him exploded and he went with it.

CHAPTER SIX

The traffic was worse than usual the next morning. It might be Sunday, but in the city there was always a constant buzz, not helped by the amount of roadwork causing bottlenecks and diversions. Alex felt resentful at the amount of weekend working he and his team were having to do, but it wouldn't be forever. He reminded himself there were many others who had to work these days as a matter of course. They would find an answer, or at least a clue, fairly soon.

Blue lights flashed up ahead and sirens blared. The local traffic news alerted him to a crash at the roundabout. The diversion sent him two miles out of his way. Kelly, another neighbour and also a close friend, was probably in the thick of it. Her ambulance shifts had her on morning duty that week. He hoped it wasn't as bad as it sounded. The amount of smoke hanging over the area looked ominous.

Thirty minutes later, he'd finally made it to his desk.

His senior technician was already waiting for him. "Morning, Alex."

"Mathilde."

"Have you given any more thought to a research plan for my gene theory? I've found—"

He raised a hand to pause her as he scanned the morning's emails. The previous day's brainstorming had led to some outlandish, albeit interesting ideas, and Mathilde had fixated on the condition of the human at cellular level rather than invasion by some unknown pathogen. But he had no time to listen, not right now. All the messages were flagged as urgent, vying for his attention. The first was one he couldn't avoid. None of them could. Georgie demanded their presence at an urgent meeting. The time had come to go public. It could only mean things were getting worse.

"Come on, Mathilde. Round up the troops. Briefing down the hall."

As she pulled his team together, he browsed a couple more messages, his heart sinking ever further. Whatever was happening had gathered speed, the number of victims appearing to double every day—and not just in the U.K., but around the world. He could see the names of colleagues from the U.S. and Europe in his inbox. There were no borders when it came to this disease. And Alex was already certain it was a disease despite the press's—and Mathilde's—attempts to assert otherwise.

Georgie Holland was already there, quietly talking in a corner to the senior consultants. They were all here. This was bad, very bad indeed. An IT technician was fiddling with a laptop. Alex and his team took their seats near the front.

"Have you thought any more about my suggestions?" asked Mathilde, as they waited for the room to fill.

"It's an interesting one, I'll admit," said Alex, "but—"

"But you think spontaneous mutation is too far-fetched."

He didn't have time to answer as Georgie clapped her hands for silence.

"Apologies, ladies and gentlemen for taking you away from your already busy schedules, but recent events demand our attention. As I'm sure you're all aware, there have been some distressing videos posted lately of those who have succumbed to something people are calling the "zombie plague." Most attribute these instances to the use of some as yet unidentified narcotic. However, considering the number of people showing symptoms, and taking into account a whole range of backgrounds and lifestyles, plus the blank drawn on drug tests carried out by Dr. Alex Griffiths and his team, I think it is now safe to assume the answer lies elsewhere."

A frozen image flashed up on the screen behind Holland, ready to play.

"We currently have twenty patients in our isolation ward. Other hospitals are reporting similar figures. And we are all following the same quarantine protocol for any new cases. Whilst these numbers are manageable, I must stress that the rate of increase is driving up sharply—particularly with the discovery of people in this state who have gone unnoticed. For example, those who live or work alone or who—well, you know. From paramedic reports, I am sorry to tell you we will have at least one hundred cases in our wards by the end of the day. We are currently making arrangements with the army to bring them here in a controlled manner. Don't want to spook people with a caravan of ambulances outside, do we?

"The government will be making a general statement tonight—they're aware of the situation, nothing to worry about etc etc—giving us a couple more days grace to come up with something. On Tuesday evening, the Prime Minister and our chief scientists are intending to go into more detail, and you can imagine what the public response to that will be! But it does give us a little more time to come up with a cause and, hopefully, a solution—or at least a view to a solution."

Two days, thought Alex. Barely any time at all considering they were pretty much stumped. Georgie was being optimistic.

"Our tests," continued Georgie, "have revealed the body functioning normally in terms of maintaining the appearance of living, but there is no apparent awareness. There are no reflexes, no response to stimuli, nothing. All we know is that the neural pathways have been disrupted in some manner leaving the victim in what can only be described as a vegetative state. They do not require assisted breathing—the lungs continue to function perfectly—but they do need other aspects of life-support such as feeding and the removal of waste products. Whilst we discuss next steps with the family, we are proceeding with a full CT scan plus lumbar punctures on all patients. I'm afraid we can no longer go one step at a time and wait for results of one test before moving onto the next. We have to throw everything at this."

Alex pondered Georgie's words. "Next steps" was the euphemism for withdrawal of life-support allowing the patient to die, but they needed these patients alive to work on a solution. It was a poor choice of words from his boss, negated her optimism.

Alex felt a low vibration from his phone but ignored it. He had to focus for the time being.

"In addition," continued Georgie, "the videos which have been shared, and those which have not, may provide us with a clue as to what is happening. We need to study behaviour and environmental factors, look at everything. We have uploaded as many as we can to the system, categorised by age, sex, and location. These will be extremely distressing to watch, but it's vital we do so. There *has* to be something we're missing."

Georgie then went through every test run, every blank drawn, displayed the inert bodies of the patients brought in on the screen. Alex was already aware of the majority of this information, but he had been under strict instructions as to what he could share with his team. Today all such restrictions were being lifted. He wondered what they had made of the videos.

"We have come to the conclusion the answer has to lie in the brain, and that is where our focus will be," Georgie said, at the end. She didn't dismiss them immediately, looking around the room as if considering her words. Georgie visibly swallowed.

Alex steeled himself for bad news.

"This morning, we sadly lost two of our paramedics. They were bringing in another person who appears to have fallen victim. Their ambulance crashed on the way back to the hospital. I…um…we have…um…video. As you know, all who attend calls, film events and…um… The medic started filming as soon as they realised their patient was someone of interest to us. Patched us in so we received the images in real time, could watch as they travelled. That video might be valuable to watch, but it will be difficult. We have flagged it so you know which one and can prepare yourself. Needless to say, this footage must not be shared with anyone, especially their families. Now, back to work everyone."

Alex's phone vibrated again. He continued to ignore it.

By the time they were back in the lab, breaking news messages were flashing across the screen on the wall.

"That's all we need," said Alex, as Mathilde pulled on her protective gear, "the world panicking." So much for Tuesday. The breathing space had gone.

"Yes," she said, "but we got through it before, I daresay we'll do it again. There are protocols in place now. And quotas on pasta and toilet rolls."

They laughed, and he returned to his desk. He clicked on the link Georgie had sent to give access to the footage. His phone vibrated again. This time he pulled it out, anything to delay the moment when he would have to watch people die on repeat.

It was a text from Anwen. The girls hadn't come back last night, probably slept over. She'd got a text from Nic asking for a lift, even though it was a matter of five minutes' walk for goodness sake—but neither daughter had responded to her messages saying she was on her way. She was going to pick them up anyway; their fault if they weren't ready.

Typical teens, was his reply. He smiled. At least there was still some normality in the world. He noticed a text from Pete. His brother would have to wait.

He turned his attention back to the folder, noticing it was updating rapidly, more and more footage being uploaded. As he clicked on these, he realised they were different to those he'd seen on his wife's phone. Before, others had moved in to try and help the afflicted. That had changed. With the growing awareness, social media had done what it does best and spread fear and uncertainty.

A Facebook post carried a video from someone in China. It showed a room packed with people standing, none moving, only the numbers apparently keeping them upright. "It's a nerve gas," said the writer. "They're testing chemicals on us." "Laboratory leak." said another.

Another post showed a group of people in America taking some form of communion in celebration of the Rapture. The post had been quickly taken down when it was realised it was a mass suicide. Nor was it the only occurrence of such happenings. Churches across the world reported an uptick in attendance—until the congregations froze.

"Power outages forecast!" declared one particularly sickening picture of engineers burning up on substation cabling. Stocks of wood and coal, candles, blankets, water, canned goods vanished from warehouses, not even getting as far as a supermarket shelf.

Stampeding shoppers were shown fighting for what was left, crushing and trampling anyone in their way. "Our supply chain will be fine," said the government, "provided people don't panic." Leaked documents circulated swiftly in response: doomsday figures, army interventions, rationing, curfews, social control. With every post came another more extreme response, always accompanied by photos and videos of the most horrific incidents. It was the same in every part of the world as far as he could see. And there was no sense of "we're all in this together." Instead, it was every man—or woman—for themselves.

The miserable day passed quickly as Alex buried himself in the reports and the posts, trying to identify similarities—or even better—a trigger.

The day buried him in misery. He glanced at the clock. Time to see what the government had to say for itself.

A "breaking news" banner streamed across the bottom of the TV screen, but the lectern in the Downing Street briefing room on which the camera was trained, remained empty. To fill the empty air time, reporters presented unhelpful—and scary—hypotheses. Locally, Southampton fed itself on rumour and conspiracy theories as its residents sought to close the gap in their knowledge. He returned to his work, clicked another file. It was tagged 'Southampton' *his* city. CCTV from a number of angles showed the ripple effects following the discovery of one afflicted, the growing panic.

The quantity of uploaded videos showing those struck down had increased. Theories grew wilder and reactions amongst the city's inhabitants more extreme. The masks discarded at the end of covid, reappeared. Folks kept their distance from each other. Gloves were worn continually. The shopping centre began to resemble a ghost town. This was happening in *hours*, not days! Shit, where was the government? The TV showed reporters waiting impatiently. The situation had escalated horrifically.

On his computer, Alex found himself watching a youth sitting on a bench, staring at the phone in his hand. At first, nobody paid him any attention. He was only doing what teens had done for years, staring at his phone as if nothing else existed. But when the same workers and shoppers passed him again on their return journeys—half an hour, an hour, two hours later—they noticed he was still in the same position. They began to give him a wide berth, their distance from him increasing as word apparently got around, eventually emptying the street completely. An increasingly common scenario. The shops locked their doors and allowed customers to scurry out the tradesmen's entrances around the back. Buses diverted away from the area and, whilst allowing travellers to disembark, began to refuse admittance to others. Alex clicked to another when the ambulance arrived to take the youth away.

A young girl was slumped at the base of a tree, her clothing somewhat disturbed. She seemed vaguely familiar. He felt an increasing knot of anxiety as he thought of his own daughters, thankful his wife had gone to fetch them and bring them home. He looked again at the girl. She could so easily have been Nic or Sian.

His thoughts went back to his brother's text. It had been a while since they'd spoken, too long if truth be told. Later, he promised himself. Once the day was done, he'd call back.

CHAPTER SEVEN

"Sorry, Mum." Nic did her best to look remorseful. It was hard though; her hangover was as bad as she'd expected.

Her mum glared at her. "We let you go to the party on the condition you came home before ten this morning!"

Nic glanced at her watch. "It's only eleven, Mum! Not that bad." She put down the glass of water in her hand and rubbed her temples. She should've known her mum would've come marching around to Jules' house.

"And where's your sister?"

Nic scanned the living room. Mum would have no qualms about barging upstairs to find her.

Comatose bodies littered the floor, one or two were sitting up and groaning. They barely noticed Nic's mum, too wrapped up in their own small bubble of pain. Discarded bottles lay amongst the bodies, the large punchbowl empty with only shrivelled slices of lemon and some unknown fruit remaining. That particular drink had been lethal. She had asked Jules what was in it, but her friend had only grinned. Then she heard another groan, recognised her sister from its timbre.

Sian emerged from behind a sofa, looking confused and green.

"I'll nip upstairs, Mum," said Nic. "Let Jules know we're going."

Her mother only gave her the slightest acknowledgement, too focussed on the dishevelled state of her little sister to pay her any more attention. With a sigh of relief, Nic picked up the tumbler of water and slipped back upstairs. Luke was still asleep in the small spare room they'd been able to shut themselves away in. She put the glass on the bedside table and leaned down to give him a kiss on the cheek.

He didn't respond.

Dead to the world, she thought. She sent him a quick text so he'd know she'd had to go and made her way to Jules' room.

There was no answer to her tap on the door.

Nic opened the door and peered round. "Jules!" she whispered.

Her friend gave no response. She, too, was sleeping off the effects of the previous night. Nic texted a quick thank you and left her. They'd catch up later, analyse the party and its success, talk about Luke. They'd been hovering around each other for so long, Jules had threatened to bang their heads together. In the end, the punch had done the talking—and more.

Nic couldn't stop grinning as she made her way back downstairs, only composing herself when her mother raised an eyebrow at her. There would be an interrogation. She glanced at Sian, who rolled her eyes behind their mother's back and then obediently followed her outside.

"You didn't bring the car?" Sian was looking up and down the pavement.

Their mum looked slightly disbelieving at her youngest. "To walk half a dozen houses down the road? You must be kidding. Besides, the fresh air'll do you good."

Sian groaned, and Nic grinned once more.

"Don't know what you're so happy about," said Sian. "You and Luke were certainly putting it away last night."

"Luke?"

Now it was Nic's turn for a grilling. She'd have words with Sian later.

"I didn't see him there," said their mum.

"Probably lucky enough to get a bed upstairs," smirked Sian.

Nic felt herself grow hot. This was not on. She readied herself for her mother's lecture and then noticed she'd fallen behind them. "Mum?"

"It's okay, just felt funny for a moment. A bit tingly."

"You sure you're all right?" Sian this time.

Their mum smiled. "Probably another of those things I can add to my list of menopausal symptoms and sufferings."

The girls groaned at yet another reference to something which had no meaning for them. Those years were a long way off. But her mum insisted on keeping them informed, making sure they knew what was coming, delighting in their discomfort. Sometimes she took "embarrassing mum" to a whole new level.

They moved on, Nic relieved they were almost home. "Go and sit down, Mum," she said, when they finally got inside. "I'll make you a cup of tea."

"I'm going to crash for a bit," said Sian. "Unless you want anything,

Mum?"

Her mum shook her head. Sian made her exit, leaving Mum and Nic alone. Mum took the glass of water from her daughter and sipped it gratefully. "Dare say you want to crash out for a while as well?"

Nic nodded but still looked at her mother with concern. The woman's face had gone pale.

"Pass me a couple of aspirin and I'll be fine," she said. "You go on up. You can tell me *all* about the party later."

Nic noted the emphasis on *all*. That meant she hadn't forgotten about Luke. Nic popped the tablets from their pack and passed them over.

"I'll be fine," her mum repeated. "Go on up."

Nic kissed the top of her head and squeezed her hand before making her way to her room. Passing Sian's, she noticed her sister was already buried beneath her blankets, their surface rising and falling with her breath.

Lightweight, she thought.

She kicked off her shoes and opened the window slightly, enjoying the gentle breeze. Nic had to admit it, she was pretty tired. A sudden tingle ran through her body as she pulled her quilt back.

Must be coming down with something, she thought, but dismissed it as nothing to worry about and closed her eyes.

Nic had barely dozed off when something roused her. A pain seared through her head, pounding away. A hammering hangover. As soon as she'd finished cursing Jules' punch, it vanished. She pondered getting an aspirin. If she yelled loud enough, Mum would bring it.

"Mum!"

There was no response.

She tried again. "Mum!"

With a sigh, she cocooned herself in her quilt and tapped out a message to her mother. Dad had always mocked her about texting when they lived in the same house, that she could just get up and walk to a room to talk to each other for God's sake.

The message went unanswered.

She debated getting the aspirin herself but felt too cosy to move. Her stomach shifted slightly, a queasiness reasserting itself from the lack of food. She texted another message to her mum, this time asking for a sandwich.

No answer.

The small gap between her quilt and pillow allowed her eyes to peer out at the room. She could see the door, closed. Usually that made her feel safe. Today, it unnerved her for some reason.

"Take the consequences" was something her mother always repeated. No doubt this was the reason behind Mum's lack of response. If it were Dad, he'd be fussing around them like anything. Mum was always telling him off for spoiling them.

Fine, she thought. *I'll get it myself.*

Nic made to throw back the duvet, but her arm refused to obey her brain's instruction. She tried again, tried to kick it off. Nothing. She tried to call her mother again, but her mouth wouldn't open. Her body had seized up. Was it that drink? Alcohol poisoning? Spiked? No. She would have had a reaction hours ago if that was the case. Nic made another attempt to move, felt the weight of the duvet on top of her. It felt as if she was being suffocated although she slept like this often enough. But that was when she knew she could escape. Without being able to move, it was like being trapped.

She tried again, sent messages to arms, legs, mouth. All stubbornly refused. She was totally paralysed.

Nic's mind went back to the videos she'd shown to her parents, to the ones of Rosie that she hadn't revealed to them. They'd have been furious if they'd known she and Sian had been responsible. Well, more her than Sian. Even after she'd called 999, Sian had worried about being caught.

And now it seemed they had been, although in a way not expected.

Sian! Was she really asleep, or was she like Nic? Where was Mum? Were they all like this, frozen in place around the house? Panic threatened to overwhelm her, until she thought about her father. He would come home at some point, find them, fix them.

But his hours had been erratic lately, working around the clock on something he didn't talk about too much with them but which worried him considerably. He might not come back today, tonight, tomorrow! He would text them, though. Always messaged them. If they didn't respond, he would come for them. There was nothing to worry about. Sooner or later, Dad would come to the rescue.

CHAPTER EIGHT

The day had passed in a haze of distressing videos, sample analysis, and discussions which went around and around in circles. It was way past clocking-off time, but he wasn't going anywhere. Not until they'd made some progress. He quickly texted his wife and then turned it off. She understood the importance of his work at times like this. The Prime Minister had finally appeared to deliver a speech which satisfied no one.

"Did you watch it?" asked Mathilde, as they made their way to the isolation ward.

She was referring to the crashed ambulance, the live feed prior to that, sent in by Kelly, one of the medics inside. "No, I…can't. Not yet. Kel was my neighbour, my friend."

"But she patched in the video for a reason. You know that, don't you? And there's a transcript attached as well, if…"

Of course, he knew. Understood Kelly's sacrifice and how he was dishonouring her by not watching the video. "I'll watch it when I get back to the office," he said. "After we've seen the latest admissions."

With no answers, Alex wanted to see the new patients for himself, not via some screen or 3D imagery. Perhaps inspiration would strike. The isolation ward was deathly quiet beyond the bleeps of the monitors attached to each patient by a web of tubes and wires. From behind his visor, he gazed into their staring eyes. He couldn't believe the number lying in front of him. None so much as flickered, his presence totally unacknowledged. Sam and Beryl's appearance had barely altered since he had first seen them. A picture repeated in the ward next door which had been co-opted for quarantine purposes due to the rise in numbers. No chances were being taken.

Brain scans had been a surprise. Areas which focussed on awareness and cognition, the prefrontal cortex, seemed to be operating normally. Sensory signals were monitored as being received, but they were not acted upon. Something was shutting the human response mechanism down. His team were burrowing into the brain, trying to find anything which had changed.

Not for the first time, he wondered if his own and his wife's contact with their neighbours had left his family susceptible. It was partly why he preferred his wife to focus on the message about drugs being the root of the problem, something less worrying than a transferrable bug. Unless she too was masking her concern for the sake of the family.

There was one noticeable difference to the earlier admissions however— the speed with which people were being affected. Only a very brief contact was needed before someone succumbed. A mutation? But of what? None the wiser, he returned to his office, turned his attention to Kelly's video. Earlier admissions? All of this had happened in a matter of a few weeks, barely any time at all. The speed was terrifying.

Reluctantly, he clicked play. The patient had already been loaded into the vehicle and he could hear its siren blaring as the ambulance sped back to the hospital. A small hatch was open through to the driver's cab and he caught glimpses of traffic, trees, the road. Kelly was not fully visible, but her bodycam displayed the patient, a young woman, lying on the stretcher with those familiar unblinking eyes. Kelly was reeling off body stats over the radio, and then there was a pause.

"Sorry," she said, resuming her recap. "Felt a bit odd there. Maybe nothing, like an electric shock to the system. We're thirty minutes away." He listened as Kelly continued to monitor the patient's vital signs. Another pause. "Christ, my head hurts. Sorry, you guys, head's pounding. Probably a migraine coming on. Wayne?"

She was calling to the driver. Alex could see his shoulder through the hatch, the position of his hands on the wheel—not moving.

"Wayne?" He could hear concern in her voice, watched her move towards the cab and then stop. The ambulance continued to speed along and he could see the roundabout ahead, the huge tanker across their path. "Wayne!" There was terror in her voice. "I think—"

Her voice fell silent but the radio continued to transmit the beeps of the machines, the roar of the ambulance whilst the camera showed the tanker looming closer and closer. The screen went blank, and Alex noticed his cheeks were wet with tears. He brushed them away and closed the file. To watch the inevitable, to know you were about to die and could do nothing to escape, was truly horrific.

He sent a text to Anwen and then to his daughters. There was still no response.

*****

Images and videos continued to spread across social media like wildfire, and those from Southampton replicated what was being witnessed across not just the United Kingdom, but the rest of the world. Humanity was being frozen in place. Communications went dark as scientists racing for an answer suddenly blinked out of existence, the ominous sign that either they, or the workers maintaining global information channels, had also succumbed.

Alex studied the monitor, finding it hard to concentrate as unease about his lack of contact with his family grew. A new case had been picked up onscreen, and the medical profession was operating a primitive form of track and trace. No apps or individual visits could be used for this particular disease. Transmission rate was of critical importance, but they continued to flounder in the dark.

"How long before we have contact details?" he asked, forcing himself to focus, for once willing his phone to vibrate.

"Operators have been tracking back his movements on CCTV," said Mathilde. "We should have an infection route through soon."

He could hear the scepticism in her voice. She didn't believe it was an infection, that there was something going on at cellular level rewiring—or rather unwiring—the human body. Alex was reluctant to follow that train of thought. If true, it was a catastrophic physiological failure, one with no cure. Believe in a disease and you could believe in a remedy. He didn't stop her researching it, though.

He sighed. "Not soon enough. By the time we know where he's been and who he's been near, those he's interacted with will be infected. You know the rate of spread. He's been there two days." Another person ignored as the rest of the world walked by. As he had with Sam. The guilt flared up.

The room was silent as they watched the video again, their eyes focussed on the infectious diseases team manhandling the youth into the waiting ambulance. He doubted they were thinking about what they were watching, more likely weighing up the chances of getting out the hospital and back home to their families before the government imposed their threatened quarantine and curfews. The island status of the United Kingdom had offered no protection. With no answer in sight, defeat hung over their department. And still people stopped moving, remained where they were unless they were lucky enough to be picked up by an ambulance or fire crew.

How had it come to this? In three weeks? The hundred admissions of only two nights ago were already a distant memory, wards overflowing, corridors full of a continual stream of victims. Was mankind going out, not with a bang but a whimper? Switched off by a god who had become disenchanted with his toys, was moving on to something new, improved, shinier. Theories had gone viral. One of the most ridiculous was an imminent alien invasion. Was it so preposterous? The disease itself, the failure of the human physiology, could never have been imagined. It was as if the genes had decided to power down their owner, their DNA. Perhaps mankind had been given an allotted timespan after all. Or there was Mathilde's even more outlandish proposal that prehistoric genes involved in hibernation had somehow come into play, a stress response to the modern environment, a latent adaptation—another area to be explored, if they had time. The scientific community worldwide had agreed to this focus. Then they had fallen silent.

Alex regarded his team, faces pale, hope vanishing. Like his own. Whilst he would not go down without a fight, it was for his people to decide for themselves. Georgie had alerted him to the nature of the government briefing expected that evening. Lockdown was coming again, a more reasonable response than before considering the nature of the affliction. If you remained in your home then at least you were in a relatively safe place, should you succumb. Nobody wanted to talk about those same people starving, going without water. The window of opportunity to help an afflicted person was miniscule.

He would not dictate to his people. For something like this, they were free to make their own decisions. It was their right.

Alex took a deep breath. "Right, everyone. Without anything concrete—and I do mean *anything*—it looks like we're almost out of time. This thing is spreading too fast, too uncontrolled. It's time for you to make your own choice. You can leave and return to your families, or you can stay here and try and solve the problem. And there is no shame in leaving," he added. "Those you love should come first."

Two of his technicians rose and left the room. Five remained.

"The rest of you, you are free to contact whomever you need to—phones are still operational—but please return to the lab as soon as possible. The clock is ticking louder than ever."

The large screen on his wall had taken on a mosaic appearance as other events were beamed back to them. City centres slowing down, stopping, as if somebody had paused the human race.

Alex was torn. He wanted to go home, find his family, but his position and work demanded he stay. He gazed down at his silent phone.

"Still no answer?" asked Mathilde.

He shook his head.

Then she reached over and tapped a small icon on his screen. "Your security cam. You patched it in a couple years back, and I seem to remember you using it as a video link when Anwen and the girls had to self-isolate and you stayed here."

Alex blinked. Why hadn't he thought of that? It had allowed him to watch his family go about their daily business, and he could at least share in a small part of it. They hadn't been able to see him, but he had been able to speak to them and the techs had tweaked the audio system so it became two-way. He could have used another app, but having them there, in view all the time, had been reassuring.

He clicked on the icon and a series of tiles populated his screen: front room, kitchen, study, bedrooms. Normally the bedroom cameras were blocked to maintain privacy, but when the house was empty, they were switched on. The only reason they were on now was at Anwen's insistence, not quite trusting some of their daughters' friends should they decide to visit on this day off from school. He had argued with her about it for some time, but now he was grateful for his wife's suspicious nature. Zooming in on each one, he made his way around the house, Mathilde watching at his side.

A lump on Nic's bed indicated someone sleeping there. It was two o'clock in the afternoon, which was late even for his daughter. He didn't want to zoom in.

"Do you want me to look for you?" asked Mathilde.

He shook his head, swallowed. "No. I need to do this myself."

He clicked the mouse and approached the bed slowly, holding his breath as he did so, anxiety coursing through him. Nic lay there facing the camera. He could hardly see her, buried as she was beneath her duvet. He noticed a small gap between the cover and her pillow. He zoomed in further. It was hard but he could just about detect her eyes. They were open, and she was not moving. His stomach knotted, anxiety through the roof as he clicked on his younger daughter's camera.

Sian was curled up in her bed. Her back was to him. The camera could not show him the other side. She was unmoving. It allowed him a faint, but probably false hope, that she was merely sleeping. Her phone was on the bedside table, its wire leading to the charger. Alex tapped in her number and watched as the screen glowed, the phone moving slightly at the vibration. Sian didn't stir. He felt Mathilde's hand on his shoulder, steadying him as he continued his search, click on each camera in turn. His bedroom was empty.

Down the stairs and across the hallway, scouting in all directions, he searched for Anwen. The living room and study were empty. That left the kitchen and the garden. He found her sitting at the kitchen table, the old pine table inherited from his grandparents around which they'd had so many happy times. Her hand was curled round a mug. Her eyes were empty, staring directly at the camera. Had she known it was happening to her? Was that why she had chosen to sit there?

"I'll go and get an ambulance to them," said Mathilde. "If I can."

The crews were overstretched, and he knew it was highly unlikely one could attend to them any time soon. Her phone sat on the table in front of her. He remembered those calls, the ones he had ignored. He had missed all of her calls, and she had not left a message except one. How had he not seen it? He clicked on it.

"Alex, I…" Nothing more. How she had managed to press send was beyond him. A final twitch of muscular control or something accidental as the body set itself on pause.

His whole family had succumbed. When would it be his turn? There seemed to be no pattern as to who would be struck down next.

He jumped at the sound of Georgie's voice behind him.

"Sorry, didn't mean to startle you," said Georgie. "Caught Mathilde as she was trying to get help to your family. Thought I'd come in and see how you're bearing up."

There was more. Alex could tell by the way his boss was studying him, a gleam in her eye.

"You've been in contact with a lot of the infected," said Georgie. "Could mean you have a degree of immunity or—"

"Or I would be the perfect specimen to monitor," said Alex, "considering it's very likely I've got whatever this is. Want to put me in quarantine."

Georgie shook her head. "No point, really. We've all been working so closely together; I don't think that will achieve much at all. Better you continue here and, in the lab, but yes, we might run a health check on you."

Alex groaned at the thought. Without anything to home in on, beyond the neurological implications, it meant some very uncomfortable and invasive procedures.

Mathilde had returned and gave him a sympathetic smile as she caught the end of their conversation. "They'll get a crew over as soon as they can," she said. "They've put them as high priority."

He was surprised at that. Special treatment wasn't normally allowed.

"My call," said Georgie. "We have few enough researchers as it is. You need to keep your mind on the job and this will help. Leave it to me."

"Thanks." He could hear the relief in his voice, felt the knots in his stomach unravel a little. His family would be safe.

"And perhaps the tests might serve as a distraction," grinned his boss.

"Yeah, right." But still Alex rose and made his way to the doctor's station.

Three hours later and somewhat sore and bruised after being punctured, probed and prodded, he was making his way back to his lab where his skeleton staff continued to peer down microscopes and gaze at brain scans and patient monitor feeds.

"I can't imagine what they must be feeling," said Mathilde. "To be stood there and find you cannot move, cannot speak, can do nothing, yet remain aware of everything. When people used to joke about zombies, I don't think they ever thought of this."

"That's just it though," said Alex. "They are *not* zombies. Their brains are fully functional in terms of awareness and comprehension, but have disconnected from any form of muscular, and therefore, skeletal control."

"Like Locked-in Syndrome," said Mathilde, returning to the subject which had fascinated her even before the current disaster.

"Exactly like it," said Alex. He had been considering the similarities more and more. "I don't think we've anything to lose by focussing our efforts on that area of research."

"And if we could communicate with the afflicted somehow?" said Mathilde.

If only they could get inside their heads and discover what they were thinking, how they were feeling.

CHAPTER NINE

Tuesday had arrived and Alex found his family had still not appeared.

"You gave me your word! I trusted you!" He could barely contain his anger. His wife, his daughters must surely think he'd abandoned them. Hadn't he, though? Buried himself in slides of cytoplasm, diagrams of proteins and gene structure. No thought of anything else. His fury masked his guilt, his single-mindedness had betrayed him—and them.

"I'm sorry," said Georgie. "It's just been taking longer than I'd hoped. We're down on ambulance crew—"

"And you didn't tell me? And you didn't send anyone to sit with them?" That should have been the least she could do. He couldn't leave them to Georgie, be let down again.

"I'm going to fetch them," he said, suddenly determined. "I haven't been affected so far. Even if anything happens to me, well, the rest of the team are up to speed. Put Don in charge."

Georgie looked as though she was going to object, and then her expression changed. "I'll set up some stretchers in a receiving bay for you and get some beds ready, but you'll have to get them there on your own. No contact with anyone else. Understood?"

Alex nodded.

Georgie had been unable to do anything for her own family. They had gone off on a cruise before the country locked down and contact had been lost with the liner a week ago. Whatever her feelings were, she kept them to herself. Alex wasn't so sure that was such a good thing.

It felt strange leaving the hospital campus. He used the staff exit, barely seeing another soul as he made his way to the car park. Only a few vehicles filled the lot. Alex allowed the old sense of familiarity to wash over him as he pressed unlock and sank into the driver's seat. It felt almost normal. He pressed the ignition and drove out onto the main road.

The streets were fairly empty. Nobody was driving at the moment, likely worried about falling prey to this unknown disease when behind the wheel. Flashbacks of Kelly in the ambulance pushed to the forefront, and he gripped the wheel tighter.

What had she said? A shock and then a headache? Warning signs to watch out for. If he felt so much as a tingle, he promised himself he would pull over.

It was a beautiful day, the hazy sun of late summer casting a soft glow over the city. He lowered the window and breathed in the fresh air. It was sharp and clear, free from the usual pollution of traffic. He avoided turning on the radio, not wanting to hear the depressing government bulletins or doom-mongering news broadcasts. Instead, he slipped in a CD, a compilation album from one summer or other, and sang along. He was allowing himself to pretend, for just a short while, that everything was normal and all was okay with his world.

He drove over Itchen Bridge, studiously ignoring one or two folk who leaned perilously over its edges, and made for the toll barriers. These were open, an unusual occurrence but one for which he was thankful. On he went through leafy streets and along the lengthy Portsmouth Road, heading out to Hedge End. The landscape of statues was noticeable in these parts, and it was hard to ignore them.

Alex turned off the music and rolled up his window. One or two folks were out and about, few going near anyone who seemed "paused." He dropped the pretence, returned his mind to the real world. At least he had had a few moments of escape.

He took a left at the roundabout and drove into the small, exclusive estate where he lived. Their avenue hadn't changed at all. Why would he have expected it to? This was something which affected people, not buildings, not plants, not other species of the animal kingdom. The latter consideration struck him, he would text Mathilde, get her and the team to look at any comparative studies or experiments. He couldn't remember if any in the UK had worked on that aspect. Working all hours and with very little sleep was fogging his mind, preventing him from thinking clearly. That was another reason he had come out to get his family, to breakaway.

Alex pulled into his parking space and looked up at his house. It was waiting for him. His family were waiting for him. Ignoring the protective clothing he'd brought along, he left his car and made his way up the steps. He didn't care if he was immune or not, wearing the biohazard suit would terrify them.

But how would you know that? asked a little voice in his head.

I know, he answered, because I've seen the scans of brains functioning normally, because that person is still in there somewhere. He wanted his family to know he *saw* them and understood.

Alex hesitated at the door and prepared himself. The key had to be jiggled a bit to unlock the front door, as it always had, a small degree of normality which made him smile. It was on the never-ending to-do list Anwen nagged him about. Something he thought he would never miss but now more than anything longed to hear again.

It was the smell that hit him first. He should have known, recalled it from their discovery of Beryl, but still it wrong-footed him. Anwen sat in the kitchen, just as she had been shown on the video. Was Mathilde watching him? Georgie? Monitoring his movements in case he broke down?

Who will come and rescue me? he thought.

With his arms around her, he whispered into her ear, told her how much he loved her. Not the slightest twitch in response. He felt her pulse. No irregularity there. There was a puddle at her feet, all bodily control had gone. She stank. His Anwen would've been mortified to have been found in this condition. She was extremely particular when it came to matters of personal hygiene.

He rose and kissed the top of her head. "Back in a minute, love. Going to check on the girls."

Forcing himself away, he climbed the stairs to his daughters' rooms. Sian first. He opened her door and made his way to the bundle buried beneath the blankets, moving round to the side of the bed obscured on camera.

Her head peeked out over the top, hair all over the place as it always was when she slept. Except she wasn't asleep. Sian's brown eyes gazed at him, their old teen watchfulness gone. Her pulse was also regular. He didn't pull back her covers. She could stay cocooned, warm, whilst he went to see Nic.

Pushing open the door to his eldest's room, he could see the little gap between cover and pillow where her eyes were peering out at him. He pulled the duvet back gently, carried out the same checks on her as her sibling and mother.

Thankful for her slight build, he bundled her up in the quilt and carried her from the room. He took his time going down the stairs, not wanting to risk falling. He'd left a passenger door open and slipped her, uncomplainingly, onto the back seat, strapping her in. Then he opened the other passenger door ready for Sian and repeated the process. As he regarded his daughters, he considered it was the first time in a long time both had sat in the back seat and not argued about who was sitting up front. Carrying his wife out was more of a struggle. She wasn't much heavier than the girls but enough to make him huff and puff. He wondered whether Mathilde was laughing at him as he clumsily carried her out of the kitchen.

No, he thought. His assistant wasn't like that. This was no laughing matter.

With his wife strapped in by his side and the house locked up, Alex turned the ignition and drove back in the direction of the hospital. The sun had already given up and hidden itself behind an increasing number of grey clouds.

It was unnerving driving back along the familiar roads. Not because of anything he passed as he drove along, but because of the complete absence of chatter from his family. There was no sniping between the girls, no sarcasm, no giggling at something on their phones, no interventions from his wife for them to either stop or calm down. What wouldn't he give for Nic and Sian to be yelling at each other right now? The videos he'd seen, the patients he'd observed, had been frightening enough, but this was beyond terrifying.

Alex pushed his focus back to the driving, speeding up whenever roads were clear wanting to get to the hospital as quickly as possible and then slowing down just as suddenly as he pondered what would happen if he froze and found himself driving at fifty miles an hour, unable to make the turn at the end of the bridge. The indecision followed him all the way back, but eventually he was able to pull in at the bay Georgie had prepared. One by one, he lifted each family member out onto a waiting stretcher and pushed them to a ward door where nurses were on standby and took over. All clad in the PPE he had refused to don.

He kissed each as he entrusted them to the care of his colleagues, murmured promises he wasn't sure he would be able to keep. Then he made his way back outside, slumping onto a low wall and sobbed.

Alex pulled out his phone, wanting to hear the voices of his family again, even if it was a voicemail ranting at him for being late to pick one of them up. He tapped the screen, hitting the text icon by mistake. Pete. Alex looked at the message. Just a "hello," not much more. He typed out a quick "hi" in response and then returned to his voicemails. Found one from Anwen, Nic, and Sian singing happy birthday to him. The tears came again.

CHAPTER TEN

Back in the lab, Alex observed the technicians. He had never seen them so focussed, felt an atmosphere so ominous.

"Okay?" queried Mathilde.

He nodded, not wanting to speak about his wife or daughters, preferring anything but that. He pushed thoughts of his family away and tried to set his mind to the task ahead. His team was busy, studying slides and cell cultures, entering data into computers and watching worrying models of spread analysis appear.

"We can't stop it," said Don. The most senior technician there, he was the one Alex relied on to keep everything running smoothly, to apply common sense when needed. The man had pushed his stool away from his bench, his shoulders sagging. His eyes were red-rimmed with exhaustion, face haggard. His words were a body blow.

"Then why are we even here?" asked Sara, obviously questioning her decision to stay. "Shouldn't we get home to our families too, make sure that when we succumb, we're in a safe place and not just stood outside at the whim of the elements. Remember that video of the zookeeper in Berlin? He'd gone to feed the tigers when he went down with the disease. Can you imagine what that must've felt like, seeing those creatures coming towards you, knowing they're going to tear you apart and there's absolutely no chance of escape? And those fires in America. To see flames coming and you can't run, feeling everything."

Those horrors had played on everyone's minds. Alex himself had nightmares where he imagined himself on one of his usual walks along Weston Shore, watching the container ships coming in on the Solent, falling victim as the tide came in, the water rising and carrying him away, drowning him. At least his family were in a safe environment, in the hospital where they could be cared for.

The door slammed open and Hilary appeared. She was part of the next shift, one he hadn't expected to show up in light of the circumstances.

"You're early," he said.

"Wanted to do a bit of shopping before I got here. Pointless exercise, though. Shelves were bare. People are buying up as much as they can so they don't have to go out again. Everyone's terrified of where they'll end up."

"What's your worst nightmare, Hil?" asked Don.

"Stuck looking at your ugly mug, probably."

The laughter eased the tension, but Alex still detected the fear. Everybody was scared.

"What about you, Alex?"

He'd had another nightmare recently. One which surpassed drowning at sea or the all-too-real condition of his family. "We discover the cure, or the cause, and we can't tell anyone. Can you imagine that?"

"Shit, that would be fucking terrible," said Don. "You're quiet, Mathilde."

As the scientists had gone silent across the globe, it had been an anxiety gnawing at Alex. *What if, what if.* He looked at his assistant. He knew that expression. The slight frown, the air of separateness. One hand was playing with a loose strand of hair whilst the other tapped a pencil against the desk. She was about to speak when the phone rang, its shrill tone causing them all to jump.

Hilary picked up the receiver, a slight smile appearing on her lips as she answered. "It's for you," she said, handing the handset to Alex.

He already knew who it was and sure enough, Evan Gardner's voice boomed down the line in greeting. The man had no time for mobile phones or wireless technology, apart from that involved in his research. He'd even turned down the chance to buy shares in Hum despite their projected return. Evan was the one person who continued to use a landline or stomp around to a colleague's office. He was, however, a brilliant scientist. One of the best at coming up with answers. His paranoia was tolerated as a mere eccentricity.

"Evan…" Before he could say anything else his friend was babbling excitedly down the wire. He could barely make anything out beyond "pulses" and "frequencies," until he said something which made Alex freeze. "Evan, Evan. Backup a bit. *What* did you just say?"

Alex pressed speaker phone so everyone could hear as Evan obediently repeated his words.

"I said, I recreated the problem in my rats. You've got to come and see."

"Have you told Georgie about this?" asked Alex.

"Course I have," said Evan. "At least I left a message with her secretary. But I can't wait on her. You need to see it now!"

Alex surveyed his team. "Hilary, you stay here and hold the fort. Don't worry, we'll open up a video chat so you can see what's going on. The rest of you come with me."

"How do you reckon he did it?" asked Mathilde.

"Probably zapped them with those bloody death rays of his," growled Don. "Don't see what bearing any of this can have on something which appears to be passed from person to person."

"But that's just it, isn't it, Don? It *appears* to be. We've been operating on assumptions that might not even be true."

The life had returned to Mathilde's face, a new energy sparked. Could she sense a link with her theory of spontaneous mutation? The theory Alex didn't want to consider because he wasn't sure how they could stop it.

The small group made their way along almost empty corridors. Occasionally someone would rush by, but there was no interaction, all of them too wrapped up in their own urgent tasks.

Alex was thankful they were heading into the depths of the research wing, away from the wards of suffering patients, away from his own family. It felt as if he had been given a respite from the immediacy of the problem.

The silence of the corridors was soothing, their sterility calming. He had been bombarded with information, demands, orders, every minute of every hour. The overload had been horrendous, but here it fell away from him and he could finally breathe. A clearer head was what they all needed.

Evan's lab was almost in the basement. Hidden so well you wouldn't find it unless you knew where to look. It had been one of Georgie's conditions in order for Evan to continue his research. Animal welfare took an increasingly dim view of the use of animals in experiments—even if they were just rats and the results could mean huge advances in human medicine. Evan had agreed and had been buried so long in the bowels of the building, a large number had forgotten he existed, jumping with surprise whenever he reappeared. On more than one occasion, Alex had heard them mutter "but I thought he was dead!" Comments which when relayed, caused Evan no end of amusement.

Don knocked on the door to the lab. You could only enter by key code. There were no windows for the curious to peer through.

As Don raised his fist to knock again, the door opened and Evan stood before them, tired and dishevelled, a mirror of their own state—but also excited.

"Come, come, come," he said, guiding them through his chaotic lab to an observation room at the back. There was nothing in this room beyond a table with a perspex cage containing a rat. The animal was contentedly nibbling at a piece of biscuit. At each of the four corners of the room stood a small table, on top of which was a miniature version of the cell towers so frequently seen in the neighbourhood.

"For Christ's sake, Evan," said Don. "You've really got a bee in your bonnet about those things, haven't you? We've got a fucking pandemic on our hands and you're still playing with your toys."

If Evan was annoyed at Don's words, he gave no sign.

"First I want you to go and look at old Monty," said Evan. "Make sure you're happy with his condition. I've got all his vitals on record out here."

"Evan—" said Alex.

"No, no," said Evan. "Now's not the time for talking. It's the time for seeing, for observing."

Don threw a sceptical look in Alex's direction but obediently entered the room. Mathilde was already cupping the rat in her hands, cuddling him against her.

"Seems normal to me," she said, holding him out to Don who reluctantly took hold of the creature.

"Yeah," he said. "It's a rat."

Alex allowed himself a quick look at the rodent before he turned his attention to the corner structures.

"I'll explain when we get out," said Evan. "Pop him back in his box and I'll show you what I discovered."

Alex obediently put Monty in his cage and the group moved out, taking their places at the observation window. Evan was already at his computer and typing in a number of instructions, setting whatever was to happen in motion.

"Each of those towers," he gestured to the mini structures in the corners of the inner chamber, "are exactly what they appear to be. Miniature versions of the cell masts now dotted all over our country and the rest of the world."

"We've had such masts for ages," said Don. "There's been the occasional scare story about the effects of transmission but nothing that's held up under research."

"I agree," said Evan. "There's nothing wrong with the masts—much as I hate the technology. It's the positioning and the frequencies."

"What do you mean?" asked Alex.

"Before, masts were pretty much put where anyone would have them. Coverage was built up but was somewhat random in strength and quality. And *that's* what's changed recently."

Alex visualised the tower he'd seen the other morning. There had been nothing unusual about it.

"The government licensed Hum Protocol PLC on condition coverage was standardised across the country," continued Evan.

Alex remembered news of the deal, a journalist on TV placing dots on the map where the masts were to go—sensitively placed with regard to environment and with limited impact on greenbelt land. The company had developed masts which, when sited at specific distances from each other, created a matrix whose stability and strength appeared to be unsurpassed. Government, industry, and the people were delighted with the results as the matrix progressed

"These masts have been coming online since last year," said Alex, still unsure as to Evan's theory.

"Yes," said Evan, "but the last ones, the ones to complete the matrix in each country were brought online three weeks ago."

Three weeks ago, when he had found Sam sitting motionless on a bench. It felt like a lifetime.

"Coincidence," said Don.

Alex's mood had sunk. This was nothing more than Evan's obsession kicking in. He itched to get back to the lab, to the real work of discovering both cause and cure.

"Perhaps," said Evan, ignoring Alex's glare, "but watch. I've scaled transmission down but kept the distances in proportion to those usually found. Monty's cage is effectively the Lordswood area of the city with us bang in the middle. Here we go."

Evan hit enter on the computer, triggering whatever process in the window on the screen. The group peered in through the window. Monty continued to nibble his biscuit.

"Nothing's happening," said Alex, beginning to turn away. A false hope, just like he'd expected.

"Wait a bit," said Evan, glancing at his watch. "Any minute…now."

At the word, Monty froze, and the group let out a collective gasp.

"And turning the transmitters off leaves the rat in the same condition," said Evan. He typed out a few more commands on the keyboard and little lights on each one blinked out.

"Can we…" said Alex, gesturing at the door. He couldn't believe what he'd seen.

"By all means," said Evan. "Leave the door open, it disrupts the field in there, makes it safe."

Alex moved quickly to Monty, picked the rat up. He could feel its small heart beating, its breath—but like its human counterparts, there was no response.

"Electromagnetic radiation," said Mathilde.

"But people have gone down with this just by touching someone else," said Don, shaking his head, reluctant to enter the room.

"No," said Evan. "That's only what it *appeared* like. What really happened was they simply moved into the same space where they would be affected. The waves have created an invisible mesh which captures people as they go about their business."

His words raised hope in Alex. "We have a chance."

He looked in Evan's eyes and realised he had spoken too soon.

"I don't think so. When people *stop*, they become a focus for the transmitters, are bound by the waves concentrating their effect, deflecting them towards anyone in the vicinity. The human body has its own electricity, easily absorbed into this growing field, escalating the problem further."

"So they are still effectively contagious," said Mathilde, understanding.

Evan nodded.

"From what I can see then," said Don, "is we either switch off the masts, which no one will believe or accept, or we find a way to switch this poor bugger back on."

Alex allowed his thoughts to drift back to all the conversations he'd had with colleagues. All the ideas which had been proposed, tested, dismissed. Each time he came back to Mathilde's obsession with genetic material.

He looked at her. "Genetic power-down. Something has caused the genes to malfunction—"

"Or spontaneous mutation," she threw in.

He looked at Monty. "We need to take him—and any others—back to the lab," he said.

"And when you do get back," said Evan, "I would strongly advise you turn off any wireless equipment."

The mood of the group had brightened, the sense of defeat gone as they pondered this possible cause. They had seen it with their own eyes, but Alex doubted Georgie would accept it so easily, not when the answer meant pulling the plug on modern living.

"She'll only believe it if she sees it happen to someone," said Don, as if reading his thoughts. "Hell, I don't even fully believe it, but it's all we've got to go on and at least it's something—which is more than we've had before."

CHAPTER ELEVEN

"Nothing," said Hilary, looking up from her last slide. "Cell structure in all of Monty's organs are normal, including the skin. No signs of abnormality."

Not quite all of Monty's organs. His brain lay in slivers under the microscopes of both Don and Mathilde. Alex was observing the images flicking up on the plasma screen on the lab wall. Some areas of the brain also appeared reassuringly unaltered—until they came to the cerebrum and the cerebellum, areas they had dreaded looking at, knowing these controlled human responses. It was there something had gone so obviously wrong.

"Here," said Mathilde, displaying an image of the helix structure on the monitor. The bonds they expected to see between the base nucleotides of Monty's DNA were warped and twisted. Loose strands dangled in the cytoplasmic stream, touching each other, causing connections they shouldn't.

"It's a biological short-circuit!" said Don, voicing the conclusion Alex had come to. "How the fuck do we fix that? It's impossible to engineer every cell back to its original state. There's billions of them."

The atmosphere in the lab had changed from one of hope and excitement at the possibility of finding a cure to one of utter despair.

"Perhaps if it was wireless radiation that triggered this," said Mathilde, "that could also be the answer?"

Alex could hear the doubt in her voice.

"Hey!" Hilary had turned her back on the discussion, was reading something intently.

Alex sighed.

She had been following thread after conspiracy theory thread, just in case. "You never know," she'd said, "might be something in it." It had become an escape of sorts, the fantastical ideas proposed providing some much-needed respite with their ridiculousness. Hilary wasn't chuckling this time.

"There's something else none of you have realised," she said, scrolling down through a series of forum posts. "Hum Protocol PLC completed its matrix in every country at exactly the same time. Only some remote and undeveloped regions—parts of Africa, Asia, the Poles—were left out for obvious purposes."

"And…" prompted Alex, wondering where this was going.

"Do you know who's behind Hum?"

"Some consortium or other," said Don, shrugging his shoulders. "Billionaires. Oil barons. The usual suspects?"

Hilary gave him a look and then reeled off a list of names. "Notice anything about them?"

Alex recognised a couple of the names, folks who'd done nothing but preach to the world about its wastefulness, its stupidity. All the time they were protected by trust funds which allowed them such a stance, protected them from harsh realities. "One or two climate activists?"

"Not one or two," said Hilary, carefully. "All of them."

"And what do your conspiracy theorists have to say about that?" asked Don. "That they decided to press the big red button on the human race—" His mouth dropped open. "You've got to be kidding me."

"They're right," said Georgie, entering the lab at that point. "Would you believe we've been looking into Evans' theory—wild as it sounds. An old friend of mine in Whitehall has just got back to me and says they've all gone off grid. Can't find hide nor hair of them or their families."

"Oh, come on," said Alex. "They've all skedaddled to their private islands or underground bunkers or whatever they've got. You know it."

"And what does Whitehall say about the timing of the turning on of the transmitters? They need to turn the bloody things off," said Mathilde, ignoring Alex's comment, giving serious credence to the whole preposterous idea.

Bad enough, he thought, that mankind in its cleverness had appeared to flip humanity's off switch, but to think it could be deliberately triggered… No. That was beyond belief. Wasn't it?

"Nothing," said Georgie. "It's just one of a range of options. Europe's the same. They can't—won't—accept the theory, although I understand one or two other scientists came to the same conclusion as Evan after replicating and modelling the data."

Unacceptable. Unbelievable. When you've ruled everything out and were left with only the impossible, what could you do except dismiss that too? Alex felt like crying. How could they mitigate the problem, protect whoever was left?

Don clapped him on the back. "Come on, Alex. Time to stop thinking about what we can't do and get on with what we can. Now where's that death ray? Let's see if radiation can 'reset' the circuit, like Mathilde says."

"There is one sliver of hope," said Georgie, as she sat down and watched them work. "When—or if—they created this solution to what they saw as a problem—"

"You mean the world's population, industrialisation, all that?" said Alex, recalling all the speeches and protests.

Georgie nodded. "Well, Whitehall thinks they might also have the 'cure' as it were."

"What are they gonna do," asked Don, lifting his head from the small circuit he was building, "send in the SAS?"

Again, Georgie nodded.

"Oh my," said Don. "I can see how that'll turn out." He continued to chuckle.

After a few minutes his laughter had stopped, but his shoulders continued to shake. He was crying. Nobody commented. They all felt the same. If all the governments had to go on were wild conspiracy theories, then there was no hope. Silence fell over them. Alex made his way out of the room. He needed to see his family.

One or two of the doctors looked at him hopefully, but he shook his head and moved on, not wanting to see his own despair reflected in their faces.

It was late evening. Not even a day had passed since they'd been brought in and it already seemed like a lifetime. The wards were quiet, doctors and nurses moving about with subdued efficiency, beds occupied by some suffering the usual ailments, others filled by the catatonic. Isolation had become a thing of the past as more had been brought in and the hospital was officially full. Alex's family had only just squeezed in before the doors were closed. The government was bringing its

Nightingale hospitals back from cold storage. Hospital? It would be no more than a storage facility.

His family lay side by side, unnaturally quiet. He kissed Anwen's head, held her close for a moment before her unresponsiveness unnerved him, then he gently laid her back down. He told her of their discoveries, the cause of their condition. He told of their hope for a cure, the lie buried beneath false optimism. He chattered aimlessly for a while about memories of holidays, of their youth, until he could hold back no longer and sobbed into his hands, trying to stifle the sound so his family could not hear him.

When there were no more tears to come, he moved to Sian's bedside and stroked her hair briefly. He told her he couldn't wait to hear her and her sister bickering again. It was true. He'd give anything for such normality.

Then he moved to Nic's side, sat and took her hand, his firstborn.

CHAPTER TWELVE

Watching the world go by and not being part of it was a terrifying feeling. Nic felt she would rather be cocooned in her own bed, the place she felt safest, than here, in this hospital.

"At least we're close to each other here," said her father. "Nothing can hurt you."

He was holding her hand, squeezing it tightly. She could feel the pressure, the touch, the warmth of his skin, wanted nothing more than to squeeze back. But she couldn't.

She had heard him talking to her mother and sister, heard his muffled sobs. Were they really working on a cure?

"We know what's caused it," he was saying. "Would you believe it's those bloody masts Hum put up? That so-called wonderful coverage you all raved about has triggered all this. No. You probably wouldn't believe it. Nor the people behind that company. The government doesn't. But we've replicated your condition in the lab. Sorry, we had to sacrifice a few rats for the purpose. I don't know why I'm telling you this," he said. "You're probably not following. And I'm just rambling, talking to myself but—but if you are listening…it is true. We *have* found the cause. We just need to put things right."

The masts? Surely not? When she'd glimpsed his face, he looked haggard. Huge bags under his eyes. Lack of sleep meant he wasn't thinking straight. Her heart sank. How could he believe this theory? But if they'd replicated it, didn't that mean there was a grain of truth in it? She didn't know whether to hope or despair. If only she could look into his eyes a little longer. He was sitting beside her bed, out of her field of vision even though he was so close. If only she could turn her head towards him. If only. A horrible phrase which took the idea of control out of their lives.

Hum. She remembered how he'd bought shares in the company, teased by Sian for this step into finance, becoming part of global capitalism. She imagined the ghost of a grin on her face as he'd turned the conversation to what they could all do with the money they made from the deal when profits went up—as they were bound to do. Her parents wanted to go to some little Caribbean island. Sian wanted to backpack around South

America. She herself wanted to go to Scandinavia. The idea of travel seemed even more ridiculous now that she couldn't move a muscle. Footsteps caught her attention.

"Oh, good evening," said the nurse.

Nic's heart sank. She recognised his voice, disliked the way he looked at her, the things he whispered into her ear, the way his hands moved when he'd washed and changed her on arrival. From his movements, she'd been able to work out both her sister and mother had suffered similar attentions.

"Checking on our patients, Doctor?"

"Checking in on my family," said her dad.

"Your family?"

"Yes. I trust you're looking after them well?"

"Oh, oh, yes. Of course."

She couldn't bear the stuttering lies.

"Do you—have you found anything yet?" asked the nurse.

"Found anything? A cure? Not yet," said her father. "We know the cause though, so that's something. It'll take a bit of time. But you will take good care of my girls, won't you? I'd hate for anything to happen to them."

"Of course," said the nurse, his voice calmer.

Had the lack of a cure given him greater confidence? Allowed him to think his dirty little secrets were safe? She felt sick.

Don't leave us here, Dad, she begged. *Please.*

"If you don't mind, I have to get on," said the nurse.

It sounded as though he was over by Sian's bed, rustling around, opening packets, pressing buttons. Then he was closer. At her mother's side now, repeating the actions. The model of efficiency. Her turn.

Dad. Stay.

"I'd better get out of your way," said her father. "You're doing a great job. I really appreciate it."

Her dad loomed over her, back in her vision as he bent to kiss her cheek. "See you later, sweetheart."

Dad.

He was gone and another voice was murmuring in her ear.

"Daddy's little girl, are we?" he whispered. "Oh, I can be Daddy too.

Oh, yes."

She started to scream, silent howls from deep within. Terror churning as she felt the blankets and sheets pulled back. The *snick* as a wire was unclipped, the one which monitored her heartbeat and sent out warning signals when she was distressed. One of the few ways her body was allowed to speak. Untethered from the machines she was completely isolated.

A pause as sounds from outside drifted by.

"Oops, nearly forgot," he said. "Don't want to be putting on a show now, do we?"

He moved away and she could hear a swoosh of a blind being dropped, the click of a door being shut, his footsteps padding back over to her.

"Where were we? Ah yes. Daddy's girl."

Hands slipped behind her, undid the ties of her gown. She felt the chill against her skin. No longer just isolated. Vulnerable. Exposed. A flash caught her eye.

"Smile for the camera!"

Another flash. She thought back to Rosie. What she had done to the girl. What was being done to her…again.

"Hmm, still not quite right," said the nurse. "Let's try a little pose. You know. Vogue!" Another giggle. "Isn't this wonderful? So many opportunities and nobody to say no!"

His hands had become clammy, his face flushed with excitement, as he lifted her up into a sitting position.

"Say hello to Mummy," he said, turning her head in the direction of the next bed. "Thought you might like to see other."

She found herself looking directly into her mother's eyes. What was she thinking? Nic knew her mother, that she would be screaming too. Howling because she couldn't protect her daughter.

His hands were back on her, pulling her legs apart. More flashes, more giggles, heavier breathing. Then she was pushed back, the bay door slamming open at the same time.

"Get your fucking hands off my daughter!" The shout echoed off the small room's walls. She heard heavy breathing, scuffles, grunts, a cry of pain as someone fell to the floor. Other voices now. Anger flying all around. Another nurse was by her side. A woman this time, checking her over, covering her up, plugging her back in.

Then she saw her father's face, felt his arms around her.

"What's this?" Another voice across the room. One of the doctors.

"It's nothing, a little fun, that's all."

A crunch.

"Hey, that's my phone. You can't do that."

"Already done." Someone else she recognised. Her dad's boss, Georgie someone or other. "And security'll be here in a minute to get you out of here."

"What? You want to send me out there? You can't? I'll die? I've no one."

"Don't worry. You're going somewhere where you can be safely locked away."

"Safe? Locked up with no guarantee someone'll remember I'm there? I'll starve. I'll—"

"Yes, pity isn't it. Ah, here's security now."

More scuffling as guards dragged him from the room.

"Alex. We need to get back to the lab."

"I'm staying here."

"Alex. We need you. It's the best thing you can do for your girls, for Anwen."

"And what if there's more?" said her father. "More perverts—"

"I'll make sure they're checked regularly. I'll patch a video link through to your computer. You'll be able to watch over them yourself as well."

She didn't want him to go. *Stay.*

"Sorry, sweetheart," he whispered. "I'll be back though, as often as I can. And I'll be watching. Make sure you don't get up to any mischief." There was a catch in his voice as he spoke, but he allowed himself to be led away.

"There you go, sweetheart," said a nurse. "You're safe now. We'll look after you."

She moved away and Nic could hear the doctor talking to her and another nurse. "Make sure you examine them. Carry out the usual tests.

They've barely been in here a day. I'm thinking he didn't have time to do too much damage, but just in case."

Too much damage? She forced her mind back to his first visit, when they'd been brought in. She was fairly confident that had been restricted to his obscene comments, the casual groping. She would have heard if there had been anything *more*. Wouldn't she? If only she could speak to Sian and her mother. Ask if they were all right.

CHAPTER THIRTEEN

Alex's temper had not improved by the time he got back to the lab. He felt sick to his stomach, imagining again and again what would've happened if he hadn't suddenly gone back to his family's room. Some instinct had pulled at him, a feeling of being needed.

"The bastard," said Mathilde, as Georgie briefly explained what had happened. "At least they're okay now."

"Makes you think, though," said Hilary. "About others outside."

"Not just outside," growled Alex.

"I'm sorry," said Georgie. "I truly am. But we have to focus on this. For everyone's sakes."

Alex turned his back on them all and went over to his computer. An email had popped up with the link to patch into a security camera set up in his family's room. Georgie had kept her promise. He tapped on it and could see two female nurses tending to the women.

"I don't want any male nurses near them," he said, not taking his eyes from the screen.

"Hey, you can't tar them all with the same brush!" exclaimed Mathilde.

"No? I don't bloody well care whose sensibilities I offend. Would you be happy if that was your sister? Your mother? You'd be playing 'what if?' in your mind all day. If I know another man is going near any of them, I will not be able to concentrate. No matter how fucking irrational you say I'm being."

He realised he was shouting at them. With difficulty, he lowered his voice. "I'm sorry. It's just the way it is. And knowing someone you love was being abused and they couldn't tell you—"

"Then the sooner we get an answer, the better," said Mathilde. "They're safe now. We can all help keep an eye on them, especially if you're called out for a meeting or something."

Alex looked round at his team and felt yet another wave of guilt—and also crushing gratitude. He had barely asked after their families. They had made their decisions and then refused to talk about them. None of them even had the luxury of the video link he was able to use. Instead, they focussed what spare capacity for caring they had on his wife and daughters.

"Whatever we do here," said Don, seeming to sense the thoughts running through Alex's head, "is by choice—*our* choice. And the best thing we can do for the minute is forget the outside world, forget the bloody conspiracy theories—I still don't buy the whole mast thing, by the way— and focus on what we know."

Don was, as always, the voice of common sense. The one he could rely on to force him back to the task at hand. It was difficult, but the man was right. The lab was where he could make a difference. With a sigh, he tugged his eyes from the camera monitoring his family and turned back to work.

*****

The day passed—another one of unsuccessful tests, disproved theories, discarded possibilities. He ventured down to see his family, sitting at each bed in turn, holding their hand, telling them he loved them and then leaving as swiftly as he could. Being near them tore him apart. He wanted to stay but felt useless. He wanted to leave them and considered it abandonment. Feelings which never went away with each subsequent day, each a near faithful repetition of the previous. The only difference being a shortening of the list of possibilities, a well that was about to run dry.

"You know, I'd even love to have an argument with Anwen about something as mundane as loading the dishwasher," said Alex, after returning from his daily visit.

"That's something we could probably fix," said Mathilde, grinning. She was looking remarkably pleased with herself.

He raised his eyebrows.

"I've been thinking about it since you said your worst fear was discovering the cure or the answer and being struck down, unable to tell anyone. Isn't that what we all fear? The inability not just to move but to communicate. To be as vulnerable as your family, or even worse, those out on the streets with no protection from anyone? Communication *is* the key. If we build a link between us now, while we can, then if something happens… We can still take part in trying to solve the problem, tap into each other whilst we work. A new version of brainstorming. Won't that offer a little hope?"

"Wouldn't want to 'tap into' some of your thoughts," said Sara to Don.

Don grinned at her, gave her a wink before the humour vanished. "We learn to blink very quickly? You know how well that'll go; it would take ages to put a sentence together."

That had been the one thing patients with locked-in syndrome could do, communicate via movement of their eyelids. Not all could manage it, but enough to allow doctors to realise the patient was still there, still "viable." Don was right, however. It was an inefficient method for their purposes. And so far, none of the patients had blinked. But God, Mathilde had hit on something. If they could establish some means of communication then those scientists who'd "shut down" would still be able to share thoughts and discoveries with the community, those who might, just might, be able to put these into practice. The clock ticked louder.

"No, no," said Mathilde. "We have the answer already. Don't you remember the project the neurology and psychology department were working on? I wonder how far they've got with it? We haven't heard from them lately."

Professor Harrison's Thinking Cap! The faculty had given the headset the cheesy title in its early days and, despite carrying a suitably long-winded name and code, David Harrison had preferred to continue to use the moniker. It allowed for more jokes, he'd said. The headset itself was no joke, had actually led to the media producing scary reports about how the cap could be used by unscrupulous types to unlock your innermost secrets. It had been the worst type of scaremongering over something which could have far-reaching consequences for so many people, sufferers of motor neurone disease, strokes, dementia. The department was researching not just translating brainwave signals into speech, they were also looking at ways to manipulate parts of the brain itself.

"Hey, even if we can't get the cells to revert back," Hilary cast a doubtful look at Don, who'd placed a rather placid looking rat in the middle of his circuit built into one of the isolation chambers in the wall, "couldn't this technology be used to sort of—I don't know—provide brain therapy?

Massage cells so they start to react the way they're supposed to? Retrain, rebuild the connections? And don't all look at me as though I'm mad!"

"Now we're talking!" said Georgie. "This is what I like to hear!"

Alex looked at her. "It's more than we had, I'll agree. But can we move fast enough?"

There hadn't been much contact between departments lately. Everybody was so focussed on their own research, they barely had time to interact. But everything was fed back to Georgie, so he was sure they'd have heard one way or another if there was a problem. *Wouldn't they?* He hadn't been worried before, but with everything gathering speed in a way he had still barely come to terms with, that was changing. The silence of a few days suddenly felt like a lifetime.

Alex reached for the phone and tapped out Harrison's number. There was no answer. His heart sank.

There was a knock at the door. Alex turned to see their director's secretary standing nervously in the doorway.

"Doctor Holland?" Her voice drew the group's attention.

"Yes, Angie?" Georgie looked irritated at the interruption.

"I'm…um… I'm… I'm sorry but—"

"For goodness sake, woman. Spit it out," said Georgie.

Angie glared at her boss, anger replacing her initial timidity. "I'm going," she said. "Accident and Emergency are infected. Our general wards have gone the same way. I went to the canteen and—well, let's just say nobody's going to be getting anything to eat down there anytime soon. I'm going home to be with my family. The latest government briefing told us what to look for, what the signs are. *You* already knew, and you didn't have the decency to tell me! I just—just wanted to let you know."

"Angie!" But Georgie was talking to thin air, the door already swinging shut.

"Briefing?" asked Hilary, rubbing her tired eyes.

Don got up and turned on the TV. They had barely noticed it before, the continual cycle of rates and government warnings had done nothing to improve the atmosphere in the lab as their minds grappled with the problem. Alex had switched it off in the end.

They all stared in silence at the graph showing humanity's decline. The Prime Minister's words went over their head. Only the curve held their attention.

"It's like the televisions in the old days," said Don, "when the tube went and everything gradually faded into this small shrinking hole on the blank screen."

Alex understood exactly what he meant.

"I need to make a few phone calls," said Georgie, heading to Alex's office. "Try to…"

Her voice trailed off as she disappeared into the booth. She didn't have any words and neither did they.

CHAPTER FOURTEEN

"Right," said Alex, trying to lift the mood. "Let's sort these headsets out, keep the channels open! It's only on the next floor. I'll go up and see the Professor."

They all looked at each other. With Angie's abrupt appearance and subsequent departure, Alex could see their vulnerability had been brought home to them. One floor, yet it could so easily turn out to be the end of the world. The risk was lapping at their door, the affliction—the infection as they still thought of it—was no longer down the street, it was spreading through the building, could be on the next floor.

He hesitated at the door. The lab was his safe haven. Yet there was no choice. Not if he wanted to rid himself of that nightmare, offer some hope to his team. He had his family to think about, his wife and daughters. Across the room, he saw them on his laptop screen. A nurse was checking each of them, changing their IV drips. They needed him to fight for them. He had to take the risk.

"Take the stairs," called Hilary after him. "And wear gloves."

He felt as if he was living on borrowed time. Why hadn't he succumbed yet? Luck? "If anything happens—"

"Don't worry," said Don, following his look. "We'll watch over them."

Alex nodded and slipped on the pointless gloves. He didn't take the lift, didn't want to end up in a small steel box stuck between floors forever, yet the stairs carried their own danger. He gripped the railing firmly.

"Don't let go, don't let go," he muttered continually as he made his way up. That way, if he froze, he wouldn't tumble down. Others in the hospital had had the same idea, and as he progressed up the flight of stairs, he found members of staff in a stand-off. Nobody wanted to give way first, not wanting to yield their own safety-net. Alex took the risk, lifting his hand from the rail and dashing around them, breathing a sigh of relief as he grasped the banister once more.

His action seemed to reassure those he left behind as he heard them count down, stumble past each other, gasp with relief as they swapped places and found themselves safe. He focussed on every twinge of his body, hyperalert to the tingling sensation they suspected to be the first sign of shutdown.

Alex pushed open the doors at the top of the stairs. Harrison's office was second on the left. Not far to go. He forced himself into the corridor and marched towards it, noticing the absence of students walking purposefully to tutorials, no medics seeking consultations. The teaching part of the University Hospital seemed ominously quiet. He hoped they were simply as absorbed in their own research as he had been.

"Not yet," he whispered. "Please God, not just yet." Then he knocked at Professor Harrison's door.

Like his attempted contact via phone, there was no answer. Slowly he pushed the door open. The professor sat at his desk, silent, immobile. *No, no, no.* A web of wires and small lights wove themselves across his skull. The lights flashed, became faster in transmission as if he'd noticed Alex's entrance and was warning him to get away. Alex indeed wanted to turn and run, but he needed the wire cap which was currently wrapped around the professor's head.

He moved closer, keeping himself behind the professor in order to see the screen of the laptop to which the headset was linked.

"Professor? Professor!"

Lights flashed and words ran across the screen. Alex tried to push down his distress. The professor's thoughts clear to read. Finally, a breakthrough!

"Done something right it seems," said Harrison.

"It works," said Alex, relief diluting his terror albeit briefly.

"You need to make others—and quickly," said Harrison, before Alex could ask him anything. *"It'll allow us to continue to support research when you fall victim, for as long as we're able, anyway. Though I'm sure you've realised that already. It's why you're here."*

When, not if. Where would he be when his body shut down?

"How can we do that if we're immobile?"

The professor's answer was a surprise although perhaps one he should've been prepared for. His contacts had always been many and varied. Like Georgie's with Whitehall. There was a whole shadow world of which he was unaware. Global corporations and governments manipulating people every day.

"They patched me in to a government research base. It's completely isolated. No one's been allowed in or out since this whole mess started. Some sort of elite science unit set up by the government as a 'just in case.' They made contact with scientists around the world to establish lines of communication. Sadly, most of those have lapsed. I think I'm the only one still in touch with them because of my headset. I've enabled my webcam so they can see and hear everything. They'll be listening in right now. They give us a chance."

For the first time, Alex noticed the glow of the computer's camera. Strangers listening and watching him. It made him shudder.

"What's the latest from them?"

"They went quiet this morning. Warned me this might happen occasionally. To allow for the possibility of temporary breaks in communication and not panic. I'm sure they'll be back online later today."

Alex couldn't read the expression on Harrison's face. No emotion could be conveyed with this affliction. Everyone's face became a mask, nothing more than a living, breathing mannequin.

"How were you exposed?" asked Alex, trying to work out his own risk level.

"Wrong time, wrong place, I suppose. I've been like this for a day," said the Professor. *"I sent out an alert about my condition, but it seems no one was inclined, or able, to pass the message on."*

"I heard nothing," said Alex. "Couldn't you have sent a message via the laptop?"

"I tried, but I can only do this—the typing and text to voice. They wanted it to remain secure so didn't link it to my hospital user account." His headset had its own special communications window, only accessible to those on its own dedicated network.

"How long have we got?"

"I honestly don't know. A week? Five days? One?" said the professor. *"Better ask your questions, make use of the time left."*

He had one question. He needed confirmation of the symptoms indicating the onset of the affliction. How long did he have before he succumbed? One day, the professor said, but when did that time start? When did the clock start ticking?

"Did you have any warning, any inkling at all, that you were about to…shutdown?"

"Yes," said the Professor. *"You don't have long."*

Alex took out his phone, his hand shaking a little as he opened his contacts. "Mathilde, don't talk, listen. Professor Harrison's affected. He's wearing the headset though and can communicate via computer."

"Professor? The warning signs?" His voice betrayed him, his anxiety asking so many other questions.

Harrison's computerised voice spoke up. *"A tingling throughout the body, as if you've had a blast of static electricity. That's the first sign. It lasts for, oh, maybe thirty seconds. Not long, but I recall it because it felt so strange."*

"And after?"

"Nothing for maybe twenty minutes, half-an-hour. Then you get a tremendous headache. Feels like it's going to explode. Again, lasts for about thirty seconds."

As the professor described the symptoms, Alex recalled Kelly in the ambulance, imagined himself experiencing the same signs. It was becoming hard to distinguish between fantasy and reality.

Mathilde did not interrupt. He could hear her breathing quietly down the phone.

"Go into my research files. I was able to make them accessible to you before I became immobile. The design for this headset is in there. Make your own as quickly as you can. There's also a link to my communication window and the government lab—for what it's worth. You don't have much time to create the network."

"Is there anything else you can tell me? Anything I can do for you?" Alex didn't want to leave him isolated and alone.

"I have a gun in my drawer," said the professor. *"Shoot me."*

Alex waited for the laughing emojis to dance across the screen. It remained blank. The professor was serious.

"You have a gun? How?"

"How doesn't matter," said Professor Harrison.

"Your family…"

"My family are gone," he said. *"I've had a webcam feed to my office. Two-way so we could see each other in case something happened. They're locked in."*

Only then did Alex take another look at what had appeared to be a family photograph at the side of the computer. It was a tablet, the camera light also on. He could see Caroline sat on the sofa, their son, Benjamin, leaning over her, their daughter, Helen, curled up at her feet. None of them moved. He swallowed.

"Twenty-three days," said Alex. "Twenty-three days since my neighbours were brought in and it seems like a third of the city is gone."

"How much of the planet has been affected?" asked Harrison. *"So many who could tell me have gone."*

"I don't know," said Alex. It was true. So little information had been fed through to prevent panic and in doing so had left them adrift. Those feeds that scrolled so rapidly had paused as updates fell away.

"I don't even know what good this bloody cap is anymore. At most it gives you a communication gateway to an affected person, but what use is that? You might come up with a possible solution, but there's no time to do anything about it."

Alex stared at the professor's head. The lights flashing across his crown.

"The gun, Alex."

Alex looked at the tablet, the immobile family. The children were looking away, focussed on their mother, but Caroline was looking straight at the camera. He couldn't do it.

"No," he said. "If I do that, you'll condemn Caroline to the sight of your body for as long as she's got left. How can you do that to her, knowing as you do how sight and thought remain?"

The message window remained blank until he typed one word. *"Go."*

"I'm sorry," said Alex. "Mathilde…"

"We've found the files and can start making the caps. Don's already got enough here to make one. We've asked for more materials from the stockroom. Good job it's an automated system."

Alex made his way back to the lab, relieved there might still be some way forwards, even though that window was closing.

CHAPTER FIFTEEN

Nic had calmed as she became used to her new nurses. The women were kind and always came in together. She had thought it was to alleviate her own anxiety about being alone with one member of staff—until she overheard them talking. Normally they were careful about what they said near the patients. Today, however, they seemed increasingly worried and their caution had gone.

"You know why they make us come in here in pairs now, don't you, Gwen?"

"'Cause her dad's mates with one of the bosses?"

It was the first time Nic had heard any animosity directed at her.

"No. Although he is, but that's by the by. I mean, at least he's trying to come up with a solution—"

"Well, he needs to get a move on. He's not done a bloody good job so far."

"Gwen! From what I can gather, if anyone can come up with an answer, it's Doctor Griffiths. Anyway, it's nothing to do with him. It's 'cause they think we might, you know."

"No, Connie. I don't know. Might what?"

"You know. Stop."

The two women were quiet for a moment. Nic could only just make out the back of one of the nurses. She wished her eyes would move.

"It's been happening all over the hospital. They want to make sure that if one of the two goes down, the other can make sure the patients are safe."

"Makes sense, I suppose. Best get on then, hadn't we? I'll see to the young 'un. You see to this one. You know I had a banging headache earlier; couldn't shift it. At least that's gone."

"Same," said Connie. "Haven't had a migraine since my teens and it starts up now, of all times."

At these words, Nic felt the terror build. How could she tell them to get out and get to a doctor? Then they could alert other nurses, if there were any left, to see to her and her family. The nightmare of being totally abandoned reared up before her.

Go, she yelled in her head. *Go and get help. For yourselves and for us!*

Nic identified Connie by her voice. She could see the woman's arms, pale against the blue of her uniform, move near her head, assess the monitor readings. She could hear the scratch of her pen as she wrote them down. The woman seemed to be okay. Nic felt a flicker of hope. Then the nurse paused and turned in the direction of her colleague.

"Gwen?"

A silence had fallen across the room. The movement Nic had learned to pick up on was gone.

"Gwen?"

"Shit." The woman put her clipboard down and disappeared from view.

Nic strained to listen. It was a good five minutes before she returned to Nic's side. The girl could see the woman's flustered expression, how her hands shook as she took hold of the IV line, removed it, ready to replace it with a new bag.

"Come on," muttered Connie. "Get this done, then out." She looked down at Nic as she said this. "Sorry, girl. I've got children of my own. I need to get back to them."

As she spoke, Nic watched her face. It was too late. All Nic could do was stare at the woman, feel her eyes boring into her, imagine her thoughts as she looked down at the patient she had failed. Imagine even more the realisation she had unwittingly put Nic on one of those infamous 'pathways'—the end-of-life withdrawal of nutrients albeit unintentionally. Then again, wasn't the nurse now in the same boat? And what if Connie had hooked Nic up, how would it feel for her to watch Nic be allowed a chance of survival as she wasted away?

With difficulty, Nic pushed those thoughts away, tried to focus on images right at the edge of her vision—the barest glimpse of a nearby bed on one side, the sense of the door at the other. Her father had not come by recently and she was worried. She was losing track of time. On his last visit, he had mentioned something which he hoped would allow them to communicate. He'd seemed excited. She hoped his absence was due to his work and nothing else. Would they tell her if he, too, succumbed?

She listened to the beeps of her mother and sister's monitors. They reassured her, as surely as the absence of her own connection terrified her.

How long could a human last without water? Three days? Four?

Her sheets became sodden beneath her as anxiety triggered her bladder to empty itself. Something else she had been detached from. There would be worse, she knew, as she tried to calculate the days she had been there. There would be blood. No, there should be blood. Her period was due the day after the party. She could always tell the day and almost the exact hour when it would start. Hers was a clockwork body, or it used to be. She struggled to work it out. Twenty-one days? It was possible that her body was merely reacting to the stress of the situation and she was just late.

Another wave of horror coursed through her. She thought back to that night. She and Luke had both been so drunk, so wrapped up in each other when they'd broken through that horrendous barrier of shyness which had kept them from making any move. They had acted on impulse. An impulse which had involved no precautions or even thoughts of them.

Tests! After the male nurse had been thrown out, the doctors had been instructed to test them "just in case." She knew what that meant: pregnancy test, STDs. Nobody had said anything. She would have heard something surely when the nurses were caring for her. Perhaps a mention of her "condition."

Unless they'd been instructed not to, it being another stress factor which she could do without. It might even be the real reason her dad wasn't visiting, unable to face her and talk about it. Did he think the child was the nurse's? That she had been raped?

A sharp pain ran through her abdomen, pushed those thoughts away temporarily as she turned her gaze inwards. Waves of nausea rose. There was nothing she could do to suppress the surge of vomit pushing to escape.

Whilst the body did not react to external stimuli, the internal workings continued as usual. It couldn't be morning sickness so soon. Something she ate? A hysterical laugh echoed round the dark walls of her mind.

Another voice. "Connie? Gwen?"

Shouts echoed down the hallway as the alarm was raised. She heard footsteps pounding into their room, the wheels of a gurney squeaking. Gloved hands and arms appeared on Connie's body, lifted her away from Nic's vision. Unknown voices issued commands to clean Nic up.

Relief flooded her as she was quickly given clean sheets, a clean gown, plugged back into the machines which reminded everyone she was still alive.

"Checked her vitals?" asked the doctor, as she shone a light into her eyes, took her pulse, quickly examined the rest of her.

"Yes. Says here she was given mifepristone and misoprostol to induce—"

"Nurse."

"Oh, doesn't she—?"

"No. And nor does her father."

"But surely—"

The two moved away and continued to talk. Nic strained her ears, picked out one or two inconsequential words, apart from one. Abortion. The words faded away. A new wave of horror washed over her. A few minutes ago, she was dealing with the knowledge she might be pregnant, and now she wasn't.

Why did you do this? Did you just assume I had been raped? her voice howled silently at them. If only she could speak! Those tests "just in case," had come back positive, and they had assumed. *They didn't even tell you, Dad. You would have got them to check further.* She felt the fury rise at his absence. *You should've been here, Dad.* She wasn't being fair and she knew it. He was one of those trying to find a solution to the disaster befalling them all. They didn't think he should be distracted by worry over a pregnant daughter. And they were right. The knowledge broke her heart.

Time passed and another nurse came in, changed her sanitary towels.

"Blood colour fine," she said to an unseen companion. "Discharge rate light. Caught this one early enough not to induce any trauma."

"Keep it down," said her colleague. "She might hear you." Then to Nic. "There you go, love. All fresh as a daisy. I'll be in and out to check on you."

"Don't be daft, Belle. And I don't know why you waste your breath talking to them. The lights are on but no one's home, if you hadn't noticed."

"That again, Em? Didn't you get the email about the Professor? He demonstrated thought to Doctor Griffiths. Showed how neurons fire up in response to external stimuli, even if there is no apparent external effect. There *is* someone inside. There *is* hope."

There was an inaudible mutter behind the nurse. "Christ. So now I've got to talk to them as well as feed and change them? What can I talk about? The end of the world as we know it?"

"Em!"

"Sorry, Belle. I'll keep to little chats about the weather. How's that?"

"You pay no attention to her, love," said Belle. "She's just tired. We all are. Cut us some slack, won't you? Now here's something to help settle the nausea. I'm sure you must be in some discomfort. And if not? Well, it'll help you relax. Hang in there, honey." The nurse gave her a smile and squeezed her hand.

Nic heard them both leave the room. She longed for Belle to come back and hold her hand again. It had felt so much like her mother's that it gave her an almost physical ache.

CHAPTER SIXTEEN

Alex sat at his desk, replaying the last voicemails from his wife and daughters. His wife reminding him to pick up some decent wine for dinner and "none of that cheap plonk you keep fobbing me off with." From Sian reminding him her phone credit needed topping up. From Nic, saying there was someone she'd like him to meet. From Pete, his text, just "Hi Alex."

The news had covered the disaster extensively, seemingly replaying the same information over and over again, like ghouls at a funeral. There was almost a gloating element to the coverage, a competitive edge between the channels as they sought to outdo each other on the fear scale. They had done this before, that other time, in retrospect, that "easier" pandemic. They were repeating it now, triggering terror amongst the population, whipping up people's anxieties. Responsible reporting had gone out the window with common sense. Government reactions, too, had lost the plot, were starting to veer back to the dictatorial. Terrify your people through manipulation of their fear and anxiety and most would obey the harshest restriction on their lives. Say something often enough, it becomes belief, then fact—even when untrue.

Alex had allowed himself to watch the initial report and then returned to his work. They could not afford the luxury of following events. He had not known at that point that his brother had been working at the site, was in fact the person responsible for causing the disaster. All those people dead due to the effects of a gene malfunction. His brother's malfunction. Left, right, and centre, his family had succumbed, but still he remained. He had the strongest sensation he was living on borrowed time.

"Alex? Alex!"

The sound of Don's voice drew him out of his reverie.

"Come on. I need to show you something. The good Professor Gardner's been in touch."

"Yeah?" Alex rubbed his eyes. His whole body felt weary, ready to shut down not from whatever was happening but just good old-fashioned exhaustion.

"We need to go back to his lab."

Alex raked his hair with his fingers. "See what's on the slab, eh?"

They grinned at each other, their old banter lifting the gloom for a microsecond.

"All of us?" asked Don, as the others paused to listen.

"No," said Alex. "I don't think we can risk it this time."

Hilary, Sara, and Mathilde returned to their work, constructing headsets according to the professor's instructions, wires and cutting tools scattered across their workbench. It was a good way of taking a break from their current problem and achieving something tangible.

"We'll have them ready by the time you come back," said Hilary. "Find out what Don really thinks of us!"

"And we'll make at least one for you to use with your wife," said Mathilde.

The two men left the laboratory and quickly made their way down to the basement. Before, they had met a number of people on their journey. This time, there was no one.

"Doesn't feel good, does it?" said Don.

"No." He was right. The absence of life, of movement, made him feel as if it was all over already.

The door was open for them.

"Come in, come in," yelled a voice from the back of the room. "Over here."

Alex and Don skirted between cluttered tables and past the chamber where the previous experiment had been carried out. The place stank like a zoo. They were nearing the area where Evan kept his animals caged.

When they entered, Alex noticed most of those were empty—except the ones in front of which Evan was standing.

"Look," said Evan, pointing at a couple of rather mangy and underfed rats scuttling around their cage.

"Yes," said Don. "Two manky rodents. And?"

"And, these two were amongst those which had previously fallen victim to the catatonia."

Alex stared. "You mean you zapped them, and they were afflicted like all the others?"

"Um—no."

He felt himself tense. "What do you mean *no?*"

"I mean, they were catatonic, which is why they were kept with the others. I assumed my assistant had forgotten to tag them properly after testing. I was wrong."

"You're sure?"

"Yes. I just didn't realise until I checked their labels as I was…um…disposing of them. When I looked at the experiment results, the numbers of rats used didn't add up. There was a discrepancy in the figures. I had two more to dispose of than had been experimented on. These two."

Don pushed ahead of Alex, his face almost touching Evan's. Anger was coming off him in waves. "We have been basing our latest research on your fucking theory, on your stupid conspiracy obsession and now it turns out you were wrong?"

Alex pulled Don back. The man's clenched fists were already rising.

"Yes. I got it wrong. Horribly wrong. But it was plausible, wasn't it? Something to consider?"

"A theory which has cost people their lives!" Don was pacing behind Alex, itching to throw himself at the man.

"This means it *could* be a virus of some sort," said Alex. They must've missed it. They'd been spending too much time going down the rabbit hole dug by Evan. He had offered a solution which had seemed all too plausible. And they had made the assumption he had applied the usual scientific rigor to his trials. They had been wrong.

"Look, I know you're angry. But consider what this means!"

"What…exactly…does this mean?" snarled Don.

"That those who fall victim come out of this state naturally."

Don stopped pacing, resumed his place beside Alex.

Alex felt a flicker of hope replace his initial despair. "Were there any others exhibiting these symptoms which weren't zapped."

Evan continued to look shame-faced. "I discovered others once I did an audit after finding those two, but…um…they were disposed of with the other specimens. I'm sorry, so sorry, Alex. I've been blinkered— Hey, what are you doing?"

Don had picked up the cage containing the two resurrected creatures. "I'm taking them to our lab where we can carry out rigorously constructed tests with proper controls and proper records." He marched out of the room.

"Alex?"

Alex looked at Evan. They had been so desperate for an answer they had jumped at the man's theory, wild as it had been. The condition afflicting the people around him was so strange, so unnerving, it demanded an equally novel cause. Science had fallen victim to foolishness. He would not permit that to happen again, despite the ticking clock.

*****

"It's not all a waste," said Mathilde, on their return. "Remember Monty? His damaged genes? Something we found replicated in the other specimens? We've got something for comparison."

"No," said Don. "That damage was done by the mad professor fucking blasting the creatures with microwaves. That *caused* the damage—"

"But there were similar genetic indications in our human samples." Mathilde was not going to let it go.

"Similar, yes. Exactly the same, no. We just didn't want to admit it, did we? Though I think we all knew. What else could we pin our hopes on?" Alex was exhausted. "We had nothing. And now—"

"Now we know it's reversible," said Mathilde. She was smiling. "Anwen, Nic, and Sian will return to normal."

Only if they were looked after, he thought. Only if there remained enough people to nurse those stricken.

He watched his assistants carefully take samples from the two survivors from Evan's lab. No one wanted to harm these miracles, the reminder that perhaps mankind wasn't doomed after all.

"We need to discuss our approach before we go any further," he said. "Sara, can you contact Georgie, get her down here? Don, we need brain cell tissue samples from those rats."

"But—" said Mathilde.

"I know we wanted to keep them alive, but we need to analyse the cortex. We can't do it any other way. Not even scans will give us the level of information we need."

"Alex." Sara had returned. "I can't get through to Georgie. She's not responding to, phone, or email. I've put out a call, not that there's anyone around to reply."

"I'd hate to be on the wards," said Hilary. "I mean, are the staff staying? Have they gone? Those poor patients."

"There's nothing we can do without putting ourselves at increased risk," said Alex. "We have to stay here, stay focussed and try and come up with an answer." He was struggling not to think of his family as he spoke. His words felt like a betrayal.

There was a squeak as Don picked up a rat and pierced its side with a needle. Then it went silent. He repeated the process with its companion. The two limp bodies were taken by Hilary and their brains expertly extracted. It was a task she had performed many times before, until she came to loathe herself for it. She had no comment to make on this occasion.

"Before we go any further," said Mathilde, "we need to calibrate these headsets, make sure we can communicate with each other. I've already set up a forum page linking all the sets together. I've also forwarded access to Georgie's government contacts and that place Professor Gardner went on about."

"Better watch what I say then," said Don. His grin indicated he would more than likely do exactly the opposite.

Alex allowed Mathilde to fix the headset and adjust the electrodes.

"No cables?" he asked.

She shook her head. "There's a wireless chip embedded in the matrix. Good job, Evans' mad idea about turning off the transmitters never came to anything. This way we can move around, work properly. Harrison was a genius."

Was? He was still alive and breathing but already existed in the past tense.

"Okay, Alex. Good to go. Say something—in your head," she added, as he opened his mouth to speak.

Hello, world.

The words appeared on the forum chat page.

"Right. Don, you're next."

The process was repeated for Sara and then Hilary connected Mathilde. There were two headsets left. One for Georgie who had not appeared, and one for Alex's wife.

"Do I have time?" he asked.

Mathilde shrugged. "That's the million-dollar question. It's up to you. This tablet has a private window. We won't be able to see what you say to each other. If you say "wife," it transfers you to the tablet. Say "lab" and you come back to us."

Alex stared at her. "How?"

"Not me. Sara. She was a programmer, remember? Wrote a little macro to switch protocols."

"I have the best team," he said, taking the tablet and headset from her. "I won't be long. I just want to— Well, I'll back in bit."

"We'll have the slides prepped and ready for you to look at by the time you get back," said Don. "Now go."

CHAPTER SEVENTEEN

Feeling slightly self-conscious with the lights of the wired cap flashing on his head, he made his way from the lab to his family's room. The research wing was silent. He occasionally saw movement behind a window. Other times there would be a shadow, a group sat around a table, a person at a door, all unmoving. He wanted to stop, tell them all they were working on it, that they would have an answer soon, that maybe, just maybe, they would come out of their catatonic states naturally. But he didn't. He had no time. The only minutes he had left were for him and Anwen.

His family's room was deserted as he had known it would be. Replacement IV bags were stored in a small cabinet, ready for any nurses who were passing and could spare a minute to nip in and change as necessary. He took out three and quickly replaced the deflated looking bags at each bedside. The waste bags were a different matter, and the clock ticked even louder. He would apologise later, once this was all over. It would be one of the things they laughed about on that holiday he would buy when he cashed in his Hum shares.

He bent down and kissed both daughters, tucking them in as he had done when they were babies. "Hang on in there, girls," he whispered. "It'll all be okay."

Alex fought back a sob and moved over to his wife's bed. He gently placed the headset over her skull, pressing the electrodes into place as Mathilde had shown him when he put his on.

Wife, he thought. The word appeared on the screen.

Anwen, sweetheart. Are you all right? What are you thinking? I wish—

"*Alex? Alex? How?*" Her words appeared on the screen. He held the tablet in front of her eyes.

"*Can you read that? Can you see? The headset allows our thoughts to be transmitted. We can… We can talk.*" Tears ran down his cheeks as his free hand clasped hers.

"*Oh Alex. Nic and Sian, are they—*"

"*They're fine, darling. I've fitted up fresh IVs for you all, you'll get everything you need.*"

"*For a little while. I'm trying to smile, by the way. I wish I could hold you.*"

He pulled her gently into his arms. *"I'll do all the holding,"* he said. *"I'll hold on for all of you as long as I can. I love you all so much."*

"Then you'd better go. Go and do what you do. Bring us back. Bring us all back."

Her words broke his heart. He held her close a moment longer, kissed her lips, once so soft, now dry and cracked. *"I'll be back,"* he murmured. *"I promise."*

Alex almost ran out of the room, unable to contain himself any longer, and leant against the corridor wall, his body wracked with sobs. "Come on, Alex," he said, aloud. "Pull yourself together, man. You're no use to anyone in this state."

He forced his feet back in the direction of the lab, wondering if the promise he had made to his wife would be a false one. A window at the end of the corridor drew him to it. Unlike his office window which looked out onto a small patch of greenery, this one was a view of an entrance lobby, a taxi-rank and the city beyond. To the right was the main entrance with the larger car park nearby. It was an area notorious for traffic, but today there was hardly anything moving. Some people sat on benches and gazed ahead, whether afflicted or in hopelessness, he could not tell. Others had paused mid-step. A few lay splayed on the ground, their belongings having rolled out of purses and carrier bags. Occasionally he would see someone scurry along a path but could get no clearer view. They should've stayed home. They'd been ordered to stay indoors.

Adults had been reduced to infants with no one to feed, bathe, or clothe them if they succumbed. What creature, in the whole of the evolutionary chain, had become so defenceless? Their brains had a lot to answer for. He hoped the grey matter of Evan's miracle rats would help them find a solution. With effort he continued back to the lab and his team, praying none had succumbed in the interim.

Mathilde glanced up as he entered the room, gave him a nod. Nobody asked any questions. There was no point.

Lab, he thought, cutting himself off from his wife.

"Here," said Hilary. "I've got comparative scans of the slices taken. This is at a higher level. Sara's working on them to magnify the resolution at an area which seems to be of some interest."

"Already?" asked Mathilde.

"Well, you've been banging on about mutations and hibernation, so we looked at the base pairings for the genes controlling hibernation in mammals, squirrels, bears, and the like. See." Hilary turned the screen towards Mathilde.

Alex expected Don to come out with a comment about nuts, but the joker of their team remained quiet. Alex didn't want silence. They had their voices and he wanted to hear them. For as long as they could speak. "And?"

"And— And we haven't been able to map those particular combinations to our own DNA," continued Hilary, "but it doesn't mean it's not there. We just need to look for the genetic markers."

It would take time. No longer years, thanks to the Human Genome Project, but it could still be a matter of months. Did they have that long?

"Following what Evan said about his rats reviving," said Sara, "I've been searching up live webcams from our zoos. Some are still online, thankfully. Thought we could see if any primates have been affected and if they have, watch for signs of them coming out of it."

It was a long shot and wouldn't be of any immediate use, but if other apes had fallen victim, then it would be a useful observational experiment.

"And were there any?" he asked.

"Just the one," said Sara, indicating a solitary gorilla on a webcam, motionless in his outdoor pen.

"There was a comment on the feed mentioning him freezing up. Three days ago, by the timestamp."

"He'll die of thirst before anything else," said Alex, thinking of the human inability to survive for a long period without water.

"Maybe, maybe not," said Mathilde. "If this is a gene switching to hibernation mode, won't it be controlling other bodily processes, slowing them down?"

"Don't think we've seen any evidence of that," said Alex, thinking of the IVs and the waste bags.

"Only because we've been artificially supporting them whilst we tried to find out what was going on. Those who appear dead. Are they really dead? Like those we've seen revived after being in freezing conditions."

Alex didn't like to think about it. "I would assume the proper checks were made on the victims."

Mathilde shrugged. "It's something to bear in mind, something to hope for—that waking up and returning to normal is a possibility. What else have we got?"

Alex gave a small smile. "You're right. It's something to hold on to. And if I'm next to go down, I want you to test that theory on me. Put me in the cot in my office, but no drips, nothing. Use me to see what happens without any intervention."

"You can do the same to me," said Don.

The rest of his team also agreed.

"We're all in it together," said Hilary. "And with any luck, we'll come out of it together."

Alex didn't say anything. He couldn't trust himself to speak.

"Here we go," said Mathilde, pulling up an image of codes, multicoloured columns and bars, a helix. "It's the hibernation markers for bears. As the largest hibernating mammals, I thought it would be more appropriate to start here."

"Now all we have to do is examine those in an affected human."

"And we've got that," said Sara. "Autopsy samples are online. We just need to search and compare. I've programmed a sequencing comparison already."

"So we wait," said Don.

"And watch," said Mathilde, nodding at the gorilla on the zoo camera.

"If you want something to do," said Sara, "you can pop into the other labs, pick up any laptops or tablets lying around. Bring them here and I'll patch them into the hospital's CCTV. Make additional observations."

"And I'll put the kettle on," said Don. "A man knows his place!"

They all laughed, allowing themselves an almost normal moment.

CHAPTER EIGHTEEN

Another day passed, all of them glued to their screens, studying sequence after sequence, trying to work out what had initiated such a catastrophic failure of human physiology. At least they were all agreed on what it was— not a disease, but an environmentally triggered hibernation response to a stressed environment. Alex had first thought Mother Nature had decided to rid itself of the human race. Now he understood she was trying to protect them, help them survive, albeit in a way they were not prepared for and which could ultimately wipe them out by accident.

He looked at the gorilla on the webcam. The animal still hadn't moved. He found the creature drew him back more and more. Every time he looked, he convinced himself the ape had moved slightly, had twitched, but it was all a trick of the mind, an expression of what he wanted to see rather than what actually happened.

Alex returned to the computer's latest readings. The machine was homing in, moving closer to an answer. He could sense it from Sara's excitement, although the woman had refrained from saying anything. She would not give an opinion until she was certain.

His mood lifted, and he allowed himself a glimpse of his family. They lay there so peacefully you wouldn't think there was anything wrong. As he moved the mouse on his desk, his hand shook. A strange sensation ran through his body as if he'd received a minor shock, a tremor which caused his heart to skip a beat. The surge ran through his body, his fingers and scalp prickling. It did not last very long.

He got up and went over to the cot, cleared off the jackets and files, plumped up the pillows, straightened the blankets, pulled back the blind. He wanted to be able to see the sky, see the world beyond the hospital.

"Alex?"

Don was standing in the doorway.

"Just had a funny turn," he said. "Getting things ready."

"Alex?" Mathilde had joined Don.

"Seems I'm out of the picture. A long time coming considering the rest of my family, but we knew it would happen sooner or later."

Mathilde stepped over to him and pulled him into a hug. Then it was

Don's turn, followed by Hilary and Sara. They held him until his head began to pound, a pain searing across his skull which would have sent him tumbling to the ground if his team—his friends—hadn't been holding him. Again, it was for a mercifully brief length of time.

"I'll get you something to eat," said Hilary, scuttling out of his office, dabbing at her eyes with a tissue.

"Last meal for the condemned man, eh?" he joked.

Nobody laughed.

"It won't be long," he said. "Sara's on the scent, aren't you?"

She nodded back at him, gave a watery smile.

"Make sure you talk to me, all of you. Don't forget I'm here. Keep me in the loop. After all, I'm known for doing my best thinking lying down."

He went over to the bed and lay down, made sure he could see out of the window. He reached across to the wide sill and propped up a tablet so he could observe the team at work on his webcam. Don placed another tablet next to it which showed his wife and daughters.

"I don't—" His mouth seized, his voice silenced. Alex had joined the ranks of thousands of humans frozen in time. Almost.

Lab, he thought.

"We can hear you Alex," called Mathilde. She had fled back to the lab, was sat at her bench with her head in her hands. Hilary had come back in with a bowl of something. His last meal had come too late. Without a word, Hilary put the bowl down and went over to hug Mathilde. Disaster was crawling ever nearer.

"Hey, I'm not dead yet! he said. *And I can move my eyes a little! No one's reported that—or observed it."*

Don blocked his view, picking up the bowl Hilary had left on the bedside cabinet. He grinned. "Don't mind if I help meself to a bite to eat. Do you? Wouldn't want it to go to waste! You can watch me!"

"Go for it, said Alex. *You know, now that this has happened, I feel strangely calm. Keep on with your work, all of you. I know we're close. And feed the information back to that site Harrison connected to. It's up to you now. And you, Don! You're on bedpan duty!"*

"No pressure then," said Sara, bending over and giving him a peck on the cheek. "I'll let you know as soon as I find something. Let us know as soon as you can't change your 'view,' won't you."

That was the hardest part, watching his team pick up the slack, the weight of the world's problems on their shoulders. Were there other teams like his across the world? There must be—the law of probabilities hinted at it. The thought reassured him.

A bleak late afternoon sun shone across the park beyond. Birds flew across the sky. He envied them, their freedom.

"More matches are coming in, Alex. It looks as though there may be something to this hibernation theory. Gene markers are showing real similarities. If only—ow, shit, that hurt! Oops, sorry, everyone. Just—"

She didn't need to say anymore. Alex could've cried. She was their computer genius, the brilliant analyst.

"Don't worry, Alex," said Sara. "The sequencing is up and running. I've written a macro to help the analysis of gene markers."

"And a 'Dummies Guide,' I hope," said Don.

Alex watched the man move over to Sara's side put an arm round her shoulder. Hilary had disappeared and returned with a gurney. She wheeled it into Alex's office. Don brought Sara in, sat her down in his chair, and pushed the desk over to the wall.

Hilary lowered the gurney to the same height as Alex, placed pillows and blankets ready, pulled up the safety bars.

"Even if we can do nothing else," said Hilary, "we can look after you, keep you safe."

Sara gave a cry of pain and curled in on herself. Don remained at her side, holding her until the spasm was over. Then he guided her to the bed, and she lay down. Mathilde fixed a tablet to the bars on her bed, linking her into their headset network.

"No staying power, girl," said Don. "Wait 'til we crack it. And you will be buying the first round."

Sara gave a weak laugh but didn't say anything. Nobody ever thought it would happen to them—until it did.

Nothing to be scared of, said Alex.

I'm not scared, she responded. *Needed a bit of a rest.*

"We'll leave you two alone," said Don. "Things to do, you know. Save the world."

The reduced team returned to the labs. He watched them work, bursts of activity as they scanned reports before plunging into spells of deep thought, sitting statue-like as they did so, almost mimicking his own catatonic state.

How long would it take?

Any news, Don?

The big man didn't move.

Don?

Mathilde turned and looked back at Alex's office, then at Don. "Hilary, I need help."

He heard wheels squeaking across the lab floor. More gurneys had been brought in, just in case.

"Stupid sod should've said something, could've got him to get himself onto this bloody thing," said Mathilde.

"His little joke," said Hilary.

With some effort, the two women manhandled Don onto the gurney and wheeled him into the office.

"Seems like the penthouse suite is now full," said Mathilde. "You and me'll have to go into the annexe."

The two remaining gurneys were already in position in the lab.

"Didn't expect this to happen so quickly," said Hilary. "We've all been okay for so long, but as soon as one gets it, it seems to trigger the same response in the rest of us. A stress pheromone?"

"That's an idea," said Mathilde, moving quickly back to her bench, Hilary at her side.

Alex continued to watch and listen. Mathilde was talking, sending information across the screen to whoever was watching them. They were closing in on the resurrected hibernation gene. There was a possibility a stress pheromone was a factor in the speed of transmission. She was telling them everything, verbally, with Hilary sending reports reflecting their studies and conclusions. Linked in to the forum chat window, he could see the government lab had not responded.

"Why don't they acknowledge us?" asked Mathilde. "Are they there?"

"They have to be," answered Hilary.

"When was the last time we had a reply from them?"

Hilary stifled a yawn. "This morning, after we sent the initial report on our hibernation theory."

"Not long then," said Mathilde. "But they should know these silences are worrying."

Alex allowed his gaze to drift away from the screen and back to the wider world. He ignored the few figures who stood stationary beneath the trees. Kept his sight fixed firmly on the sky, the birds flying. How long before they, too, fell?

He continued to watch as day gave way to night, barely registered the moment he lost the last capacity of control of his body—his eyes refusing to change their focus. Alex continued to gaze at the sky.

Hey, guys. I can't see you anymore. You told me to tell you when that happened.

There was no answer.

Guys.

He had no way of seeing what was being written on his tablet—or indeed if anything was. The lab was silent apart from the occasional beep and whirr of the analytical machines.

The moon shone in on his face, its luminescence dazzling. Unable to close his eyes, he could only stare back at the glowing orb.

I see the moon, he thought,

and the moon sees me.

God help the world

and God help me.

… God help us all.

Out in the corridor, he could hear footsteps, voices. And then they faded away. Like Rip Van Winkle, humanity had fallen asleep. A modern version of the fairy tale. But would they have a happy ending? Alex could only pray. A prayer that seemed to be answered when he felt gentle fingers turn his face, allowing him to read the tablet.

"Thought you'd been quiet," said Mathilde.

Are you the last?

"In this lab, yes," said Mathilde, reading his words. "I wanted to come over sooner but things have been happening—"

Things? What things?

"A miracle happened. I managed to get through to the World Health Organisation! They've got secure labs in Geneva and so far, none of their staff are affected. We've been discussing the faulty hibernation gene and working on an enzyme to turn it off. They're almost there!"

So quickly? How is that possible?

"Computers, the genome map, brainstorming… I don't know. I'm just glad. And would you believe our own biochem lab is still manned! A couple of techs down there are having a go at replicating Switzerland's solution. As soon as it's ready, they're going to bring it up to us."

You believe this will work? That it will save us?

"Some of us," said Mathilde.

He was glad he couldn't see her face. He knew what she meant.

So many were currently without food, water, or even shelter due to the circumstances of their pausing. It would be hard coming back from that. A small window in the corner of the screen showed his family in their hospital beds. The care they had received, they had a chance. There was still time for them.

And there are those who will wake up naturally. Remember the rats? Not many, but some. What was it in their physiology which allowed this to happen? Or was it just luck?

Mathilde remained silent.

Mathilde? You okay?

"Huh? Oh, sorry. It's just being on my own. It's scary."

Don: *I'm here.*

Hilary: *So am I.*

Sara: *And me.*

Messages from the whole team scrolled down their chat window

Alex: *You're not alone, Mathilde.*

Alex felt Mathilde squeeze his hand and then listened as her footsteps took her away from them. It was still a race against time, but the world would be woken from its sleep. His body twitched. He blinked. Not just the rats could come back.

ABOUT THE AUTHOR

Stephanie Ellis' poetry has been published in the *HWA Poetry Showcase Volumes VI, VII and VII*, Black Spot Books *Under Her Skin* and online at Visual Verse. She has also co-written a collection of found poetry, *Foundlings*, with Cindy O'Quinn based on the work of Alessandro Manzetti and Linda D. Addison. A gathering of her dark twists on traditional nursery rhymes can be found in the collection, *One, Two, I See You.*

Stephanie Ellis writes dark speculative prose and poetry and has been published in a variety of magazines and anthologies, the most recent being Scott J. Moses' *What One Wouldn't Do*, Demain Publishing's *A Silent Dystopia* and Brigids Gate Press' *Were Tales.* Her longer work includes the novel, *The Five Turns of the Wheel*, and the novellas, *Bottled* and *Paused.* Her short stories can be found in the collections, *The Reckoning*, and *As the Wheel Turns.* She is co-editor of Trembling With Fear, HorrorTree.com's online magazine, and also co-edited the *Daughters of Darkness* anthologies. She is an active member of the HWA and can be found at stephanieellis.org and on twitter at @el_stevie.

ACKNOWLEDGMENTS

I haven't always had the chance to properly thank all the people who've supported me on my writing journey, including my own family. Their support in allowing me the freedom to focus completely on my writing career is treasured. To Geraint, and to our three children (now wonderful young adults) Bethan Dylan and Rhonwen, thank you for taking this seriously and putting up with a few burnt dinners as a result.

Nor would *Paused* be what it is without the feedback of my fantastic beta readers, Alyson Faye, Kev Harrison and Shane Douglas Keene. All three gave valuable feedback and helped shape it into the novella you now hold—as did my first editor Kenneth W. Cain. I've worked with him on three books and a couple of short stories and his advice has been timely and invaluable. Whilst this book is now with the fantastic folk at Brigids Gate Press, it would be remiss not to thank Ken McKinley of Silver Shamrock for giving me the opportunity to share my work with a wider audience.

There are also those who have continually backed me in so many ways and become friends in the process. There are a number of these, but in particular, I would like to thank Steve Ventura (of Brigids' Gate Press), T.C. Parker, Kev Harrison (again), Cindy O'Quinn, Kim Napolitano, Max Stark, Stuart Conover (of Horror Tree), Wayne Fenlon, Shane Douglas Keene and Theresa Derwin.

I mentioned Alyson Faye above, but I would like to say thank you for being a true real-life friend and for sharing the trials and tribulations of our chosen career. A wonderful writer in her own right, please go and check her out.

And to everyone who's ever read my work, thank you. It means the world.

CONTENT WARNINGS

Assault
Sexual assault
Suicide
Abortion

MORE FROM BRIGIDS GATE PRESS

Visit our website at: www.brigidsgatepress.com

Coming July 2022

Arthur, whose life was devastated by the brutal murder of his wife, must come to terms with his diagnosis of dementia. He moves into a new home at a retirement community, and shortly after, has his life turned upside down again when his wife's ghost visits him and sends him on a quest to find her killer so her spirit can move on. With his family and his doctor concerned that his dementia is advancing, will he be able to solve the murder before his independence is permanently restricted?

A Man in Winter examines the horrors of isolation, dementia, loss, and the ghosts that come back to haunt us.

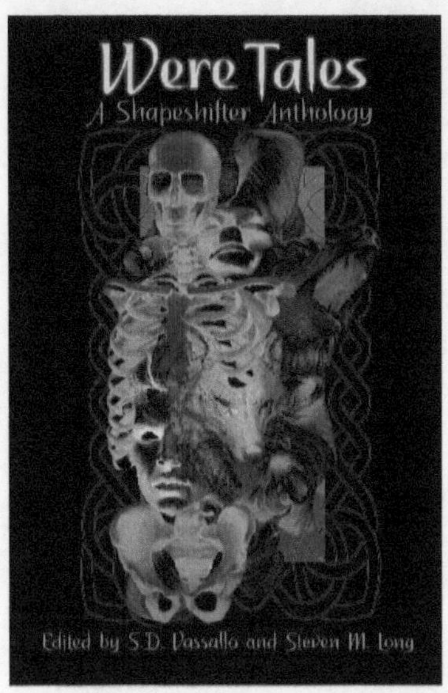

Available on Amazon

Werewolves. Berserkers. Kitsune. From the most ancient times, tales have been told of people who transform into beasts. Sometimes they're friendly and helpful. Sometimes they're tricksters, playing jokes on their hapless victims. And sometimes, they're terrifying.

Available where books are sold

A Quaint and Curious Volume of Gothic Tales; 23 stories of madness, pain, ghosts, curses, unspoken secrets, greed, murder, and one of the creepiest collections of dolls ever. Ranging from traditional gothic themes to more modern tropes, this anthology is sure to please the reader…and send a cold shiver or two down their spine.

So, come on in; enter the parlor, find a place by the fire, and experience the beautiful, dark, and occasionally heartbreaking stories told by the authors. The editor, Alex Woodroe, has passionately and carefully curated a powerful volume of stories, written by an amazing and diverse group of contemporary women writers.

Available on Amazon

Sing O Muse, of the rage of Medusa, cursed by gods and feared by men…

From the mists of time, and ages past,
The muses have gathered; hear now their songs.

A web of revenge spun 'neath the moon;
A poet's wife who breaks her bonds;
A warrior woman on a quest of honor;
A painful lesson for a treacherous heart;
A goddess and a mortal, bound together by the travails of motherhood.
And more.

Listen to the muses, as they sing aloud…HER story.

Musings of the Muses is an anthology of 65 stories and poems based on Greek myths. The stories and poems, like the myths themselves, cast long shadows of horror, fantasy, love, betrayal, vengeance, and redemption. This anthology revisits those old tales and presents them anew, from her point of view.

Coming September 2022

During the Spring Equinox underneath London, four people enter the caves, but only one will survive. Each trespasser must battle their own demons before facing the White Lady who rises each year to feed on human flesh.

Published May 2022

Welcome to the Weald.

The Five Turns of the Wheel has begun. With each Turn, blood will be spilled, and sacrifices will be made. Pacts will be made…and broken. Will you join the Dance?

In the Weald, the time has come for the Five Turns of the Wheel. Tommy, Betty and Fiddler, the sons of Hweol, Lord of Umbra, have arrived to oversee the sacred rituals…rituals brimming with sacrifice and dripping with blood.

Megan Wheelborn, daughter of Tommy, hatches a desperate plan to free the people of the Weald from the bloody and cruel grip of Umbra, and put an end to its murderous rituals. But success will require sacrifice and blood as well. Will Megan be able to pay the price?